SEX OF THE MIDWEST

Also by Robyn Ryle

Fair Game
Throw Like a Girl, Cheer Like a Boy
She/He/They/Me: For the Sisters, Misters and Binary Resisters

Sex of the Midwest

---

a novel in stories

Robyn Ryle

 galiot press

Sex of the Midwest
a novel in stories

First published in 2025 by Galiot Press

Galiot Press
PO BOX 1406
Arlington, MA 02474

galiotpress.com
@galiotpress

This is a work of fiction. Names, characters, places, and incidents either are the product of the author's imagination, or are used fictitiously. Except where actual locations or historical events are described or referred to, any resemblance to actual persons, living or dead, events, or locales, is entirely coincidental.

ISBN: 979-8-9989547-0-2

Design by Euan Monaghan
Printed in the United States of America

"A hundred books could not capture a single village.
That's not a denigration, that's a testament."
— Niall Williams, *This Is Happiness*

Invitation to Participate

"Invitation to Participate: Sexual Practices in a Small Midwestern Town." As subject lines went, it left a lot to be desired. It wasn't surprising that the email ended up in the spam folders of half the people in Lanier, and there it remained, undiscovered. Another fifth went to email addresses that no one checked or had long since forgotten the passwords for, and so these people, too, were saved the shock or titillation or outrage.

The other three thousand or so residents of Lanier, Indiana, population 12,234, woke up one morning in January 2024, to fog on the river and a strange email in their inbox. If they lived downtown, like Nancy, they read the subject line while a barge horn sounded out the window.

"They should have gotten the 'study' part in there somewhere," Nancy whispered to herself.

She stood at her kitchen island, alone in the shotgun house she'd downsized to last year, before the market had gone crazy. She couldn't afford to buy the house now, even though it was only 1,500 square feet and on the East Side, where life downtown was still, well, interesting. Nancy was glad all the poor people and the weirdos hadn't been gentrified out yet. Someone had stolen one of her patio chairs already, as well as a massive concrete pineapple planter and the carefully shaped boxwood planted in it. She wondered about the fate of the boxwood, but it was the loss of the pineapple that hurt.

"Well, I could tell you a thing or two about sexual practices in a small town," Nancy said.

She thought about Stan, which she did every morning, though he'd been dead fifteen years now. Her shotgun house had a spare room, accessed through a steep and twisted set of stairs at the very back of her closet, hidden behind the dresses she hadn't worn in twenty years. The grandkids loved those stairs. Stan would've liked it too. The idea of that secret hidden in the ceiling just above their bed . . . Oh, the things she and Stan might have gotten up to in such a room.

Nancy allowed herself a moment to imagine Stan across from her, a sly grin on his face, as they talked about the email. Then she blew on her coffee and moved on to checking her texts. She wasn't afraid of sex, but not this early in the morning, for God's sake.

Loretta was at work at the health department when the email arrived, the alert on her computer dinging in the quiet office. She was happy to see the email with its lurid subject line. She clicked the link immediately. She clicked it joyfully. She clicked it ecstatically and with full cognizance of the multiple warnings from the lone IT guy who served the whole county government and could not convince them to use two-factor authentication even if it made them a sitting target for ransomware. *Bring on the ransomware!* was Loretta's attitude. She said a small prayer to the hacker gods and gave her ergonomic mouse an extra twirl before settling the arrow onto the link.

But all that appeared was an official-looking website with an informed-consent statement. She went back to the email to see who else had gotten it, but the other addresses were hidden.

"Well, that's no fun," she mumbled. She went back to her contemplation of hot dog carts and sabotage.

Loretta was in charge of food safety and inspection. She hated food in all its facets and manifestations. She hated the farmer's market with its jams and jellies made in dark and suspect home kitchens. She hated the restaurants that always smelled the same, no matter how different their menus were. She hated food trucks, but above all, she hated the hot dog guy.

The hot dog guy was the reason she was at the office that early on a Monday morning. A "concerned citizen" had asked the mayor what sort of permits and regulations were in place for the hot dog cart that had started showing up at all the events downtown. The mayor had forwarded it to the city lawyer, the lawyer to the county council, the county council to Loretta.

"There are no damn permits or regulations," she'd wanted to email back. But that would not have put an end to it. Instead, she was sitting in her office researching what regulations she could use to drive the hot dog guy out of town altogether, instead of having to write a new policy. They weren't New York, after all. They didn't need a hot dog cart. Even a simpleton could make their own hot dog.

In his house on the Hilltop, Don Blankman took one look at the email and its subject line and went to Facebook, where he posted, "Who's responsible for this filth?" But he didn't know how to include a screenshot of the email itself, so people were confused as to what specific filth he was referring to.

Joyce Blankman, Don's wife, didn't see the email at all. She didn't have email on her phone, and she was in the sunroom when it arrived, painting and daydreaming about Paris. She didn't know the survey existed until she saw Don's Facebook post, which she made a special point not to like.

Rachel, who tended bar at the Main Street Saloon, deleted the email without reading it until Charlie told her later that he'd gotten the same message, at which point she fished it out of her trash folder to see what all the fuss was about. Rachel's stepdaughter, Sam, didn't see the email either. She was Gen Z and well-schooled in the practice of ignoring of all emails.

By the next day, the email was being rescued from spam and trash folders all over town, but only one person had filled out the survey, so only one person knew the questions that lay ahead.

Don Blankman Saves the Youth of America

The junior high was crawling with STDs and, by God, Don Blankman was going to do something about it.

The STDs probably had to do with that email, the one that had gone to everyone in town. "Invitation to Participate: Sexual Practices in a Small Midwestern Town," the subject line had read. A survey about sex, of all things. Maybe the STDs had to do with the survey and maybe they didn't. Don would get to the bottom of it, one way or another.

Don Blankman was up and moving early Tuesday morning after the email arrived, riding his golf cart down the hill to Main Street and then shuffling toward the coffee shop. He walked bent over, one long arm reached down to haul his oxygen tank behind him like a small, metallic child, because Don Blankman had gotten the Covid, and bad. He got the Covid extra bad and everyone at West Lanier Church had prayed for him, and his brother had smuggled him in some ivermectin, which the doctor refused to even consider, but who cares. It had saved his life. It had worked. Well, it had, but it hadn't. Best to say it'd worked, but not totally. He was alive, but alive with an oxygen tank for a new best friend and on the waitlist now for a new lung, which everyone at West Lanier Church would go on praying for him to get real quick.

Don wasn't supposed to get the Covid bad like that. He didn't have any of those underlying conditions. He wasn't asthmatic or fat. He was tall and lanky, and until his knee blew out last year, he'd played basketball every Saturday up at the college gym with the other geezers.

It didn't matter though, because a new lung would fix him right up. In the meantime, there was the den of vice and loose morals that the junior high had become and that would have to be taken care of without the benefit of a shiny new lung.

The story about the STDs at the junior high hadn't made the local paper, of course. Don Blankman understood that you always had to dig deeper for the truth. Know your power and you're halfway to victory. That's what he told his ballers. What he *used* to tell his ballers. He didn't coach the college basketball team anymore. He had quit before the Covid, so it had not taken that away from him. But they'd gone to conference semifinals twice during his twenty years. That was a legacy. People in Lanier knew who Don Blankman was. He was the best basketball coach in the history of the college. Not the guy with the oxygen tank. He would not let that be his legacy. And soon, they'd know him as the savior of Lanier's youth.

>>

Don settled himself at his regular table at the coffee shop on the corner of East and Main, which since he'd retired had become the geographic center of his universe. Except for the two months he was in the hospital with the Covid, he was at the coffee shop every morning at seven. It was not, like his wife, Joyce, said, because he was lonely. He wasn't lonely. There was business he needed to get done and the coffee shop was where it happened.

"How did something like this happen in Lanier?" Don asked. George was already at their table, next to Jackson, who had probably been there since seven. That was when he usually rounded in after he got off work at the auto parts factory. Jackson was Black, but he was from Lanier and he took good care of his sister and her kids, who lived in one of the little shotgun houses around the block from the coffee shop, so Jackson was okay. Jackson was barely Black. He'd never brought up any of that Black Lives Matter bullshit. Not once, even when those kids from the college were demonstrating on the corner by the courthouse every single day that summer, even though Jackson was one of fifty-six total Black people in the town, so how could Lanier have a problem with all that? Still, those kids had been out there with their signs. At least, that's what Joyce had told him. Don had been in the hospital then, though even now, months later, half a dozen of them still showed up on the corner some Fridays at noon and what the hell did they hope to accomplish? Did anyone in Lanier besides the six of them give a shit about that stuff?

"What email?" Jackson asked.

"That email about sex everyone got." Don breathed in and out. In and out in long breaths, like the respiratory therapist had told him. There was a right way to breathe. Or at least if he believed his spacey, pink-haired respiratory therapist, there was.

"About sex," Jackson said.

Don watched Jackson's eyes shift from him to the window and back.

"Oh, my niece was talking about that." George nodded and his head of thick white hair flopped around. Who had hair that full at eighty? What trick was George up to with that hair? In fact, what tricks was he up to in general? He hadn't gotten Covid at all, let alone had to go to the hospital, which Don suspected was because he'd hid out in that apartment of his above the chocolate shop, the women who worked there bringing him cappuccinos from the coffee shop and sandwiches from Bailey's. George had lived like a king through Covid and the bastard didn't even go to church.

"It was about sex at the junior high?" Jackson asked.

Don watched Jackson's eyes follow the people out on the sidewalk.

"No, no." He glanced at the table beside theirs. Jackson's voice carried and every sound in the coffee shop echoed against the tall, exposed ceilings. "I heard about the STDs at the junior high from somewhere else."

He took a sip of his coffee and waited for George or Jackson to ask where he'd heard about the STDs. They did not.

George leaned toward Don across the table. Don leaned away. George could have Covid now. Finally, George could have Covid. It wasn't like the damn thing had disappeared. Don's doctor had told him if he caught Covid again, he was dead. Dead, with his one bum lung. Just dead. The doctor had said it over and over again until he'd made Joyce cry.

"What's an STD?" George asked.

"Oh, forget it, George." Don shook his head as if George's ignorance was deep and shameful. He gave up and changed the subject. "What are the Colts going to do about their quarterback problem?"

>>

"What's an STD?" Don had asked Joyce that weekend when she'd first told him about the situation at the junior high.

Joyce was the counselor at the high school, though she had started at the junior high and was still friends with all the people down there, which was how she knew about the STDs.

"Sexually. Transmitted. Disease," Joyce had said in the same voice she'd used to explain things to their kids when they were little.

She used that voice more often with Don since the hospital, like he'd come out with dementia or was suddenly hard of hearing. "Chlamydia, specifically." She tapped her fingers against their kitchen table. "Can you imagine? All those children survived all this nonsense only to get chlamydia."

"All this nonsense" was how they referred to the pandemic in their household, including Don's two months in the hospital and his oxygen tank and the way Joyce carried her cell phone clutched against her chest all day long, waiting for the call that would tell them a new lung was available. It was all a lot of nonsense and Don sure as hell wasn't going to call it a pandemic.

"Well, what are they going to do about it?" Don banged his hand on the kitchen table, as much because of the fear in his wife's eyes as because the kids at the junior high were all humping like diseased rabbits. He thought the fear in Joyce's eyes would kill him long before his bad lung or Covid did.

Joyce shook her head. "The nurse wanted to go into all the homerooms and talk to them about STDs, but the principal said that would cause more trouble than it was worth."

"How does he figure?"

"Well, it would be sex education, wouldn't it? Parents get all in an uproar about sex education."

"What those kids need is a good kick in the pants." Don reached for the handle of the oxygen tank and pulled it closer. He was getting upset and that made it harder to breathe. The tank was cold against the palm of his hand and he'd come to find that comforting.

"It's not your problem, Don," Joyce said. "Leave it be."

"I cannot," Don said. He would not.

>>

Don Blankman lay in the spare bed alone on Tuesday night, coughing and wondering what could be done about the sex maniacs at the junior high. He couldn't sleep in the same bed as his wife anymore. Well, Joyce had said it was fine, he could stay in their bed, but what kind of asshole would he be then? Since the Covid, he didn't sleep through the night. He woke up over and over to the feeling that he was suffocating. That he would never be able to draw enough air into his lungs again.

Some of this was real. He was getting less oxygen, what with his cheese-holed lung. Joyce had bought one of those pulse oximeters to confirm this, but Don didn't need a machine to tell him about the ways in which his body was failing him.

Some of the breathing problems were from anxiety, which was common for Covid patients, the respiratory therapist had told him. In Don's nightmares, he was back in the hospital, on the Covid ward again, where all faces disappeared. In those endless weeks, everyone had been masked. Everyone was sealed up tight. Lying in his hospital bed, he'd felt a craving then for faces that was physical and every bit as painful as each ravaged breath he took.

At any rate, he couldn't put Joyce through his tossing and turning all night, his long limbs flailing until there was no room left for her in the bed. Or the gasping when he woke and fumbled for the oxygen mask. The complicated typology of coughs he'd catalogued and memorized, like he was studying for an exam. The detailed diagram of where it hurt now and where it would hurt later. Sometimes when he wasn't coughing, he felt lost, like that full-body seizure had become his natural state of being. The coughing was his constant companion through the long, sleepless nights.

Don Blankman taught his players to always make the best of a bad situation, so that was what he was trying to do with his lack of sleep. The spare bedroom looked out onto the road that wound up the hillside out of Lanier and the streetlight illuminating the dark curves. Every night since he had moved there with his oxygen tank, Joyce pulled the shutters closed to block out the streetlights. Before he went to bed, he pulled them back open. No sleep was going to happen. He might as well study the view as he lay there.

That night, he at least had something besides his coughing to think about. George and Jackson at the coffee shop had been no help. Joyce was right that sex education was not the answer. It was a problem of moral slippage. What would teaching them how to use a condom do for that? Nothing.

Something had to be done.

>>

At the coffee shop on Wednesday morning, George worked hard with the plastic knife to spread cream cheese on his bagel, shaking the table and Don's coffee in the process.

"You should run for the school board," George said.

Don watched George smear the cream cheese all nice and thick on the first half of the bagel, leaving one tiny dab for the second half. This happened every morning and George was surprised and dismayed every single time.

"The school board?" Don had already finished his donut, which required no cream cheese whatsoever. He picked up his coffee to keep it from spilling.

"Oh, yeah, there's a vacancy," Jackson said. He never had anything but coffee in the mornings. Don suspected his sister fixed him breakfast when he got off work, rising every morning to make her brother bacon and eggs. He bet it was good, too, and wondered if there was any way he could get invited. Joyce had always been flustered by breakfast as a meal. The fanciest thing he got from her was microwave pancakes, which tasted like cardboard.

"You could do something if you were on the school board." George scraped the knife into the little plastic tub of cream cheese, but that didn't change the fact that it was empty.

"That's an awful lot of trouble," Don said. But he could see the yard signs now. "Blankman for School Board." They'd be red, white, and blue, of course. Maybe with an eagle. Would an eagle be too much?

"Naw, you'd be a shoo-in," Jackson said.

"You said someone has to do something." George gave up on the cream cheese. "School board makes the most sense."

Don brushed the seeds from George's bagel off the table. "Politics, huh?"

"Just the school board," George said.

"Still, it's elected," Jackson said.

Don felt his breath go tight. From excitement, maybe, though fear was all he'd felt for so long it was hard to know the difference. He would not reach for the oxygen mask in the coffee shop though. He could tough it out. He'd toughed out a lot in his sixty-seven years.

Joyce wouldn't like him running for the school board, though maybe she wouldn't notice. She was so much busier these days with a round of activities that did not include Don. Still, if she noticed, she would try to talk him out of it. And he didn't like that it had been George's idea, but no one else had to know that.

"I'd need Nancy's endorsement." He was talking mostly to himself. Jackson and George had moved on to the eternal hopes for a winning Lanier High football season.

If he got Nancy's blessing, maybe he could pull it off. Maybe he could do something, bum lung or no. His time wasn't up yet.

>>

Even though he lived in a town of only twelve thousand people, it was surprisingly hard to find Nancy, let alone get her endorsement.

He tried messaging her on Facebook first. A day later, he'd heard nothing and that pace was not going to cut it. He needed to move fast. Time was of the essence.

"Oh, I don't think she looks at Facebook much." Joyce sat at the breakfast table, flipping through the latest pictures of the grandkids on her phone. She tilted the screen toward Don every few seconds so he could smile and nod, even though every single picture looked exactly the same. He kept that thought to himself.

"I hardly ever see Nancy on Facebook." Joyce's reading glasses perched on the end of her nose.

"Well, why not?"

Joyce shrugged and went on flipping through her photos.

Don spent an average of three hours and twenty-three minutes per day on Facebook. He knew this because one of the grandkids had stopped posing for pictures long enough to show him where his phone tracked these things, which was not information Don either wanted or needed to know.

"Wow, Grandad." Ben was eleven and had long hair, which he assured Don was not at all girly, but what all the great athletes did now. It improved their "flow," whatever that was. "You must really like Facebook."

Well, why wouldn't he? There was a lot of useful information on there if you knew where to look, and Don did. Why wasn't Nancy on there, too? What amazing things was she doing with that extra three and a half hours of her day?

"She might have even canceled her account." Joyce took a sip of coffee, her lips lining up perfectly with the lipstick stain that was now a permanent feature of her favorite cup.

Joyce and Nancy didn't run in the same social circles. Joyce had grown up out in the county, just past Deputy, while Nancy had been a Lanier girl through and through. Her uncle had owned the old button factory that was the big chain hotel now, though Nancy hadn't gotten any of that money.

Fancy Nancy. That was what Joyce called her. When Don told her he'd need Nancy's endorsement, Joyce had laughed. "Good luck with that," she said. She'd shot him a look that suggested she was going to enjoy watching him try. And fail.

Nancy had been school superintendent for over twenty years. She had taken over when Mike Bowling died. She'd been Mike's assistant. She never would have been elected outright. But once she was in that office, she could sure get reelected. Over and over again. She'd never lost. She resigned when she decided it was someone else's turn, like that was the most natural thing imaginable.

Don had served on the library board with Nancy for a year back in the '90s. Their boys had played on the same Little League team.

He'd known Stan too. *Stan Stayed In*. That was what Joyce called him. Nancy was hardly ever at home and Stan always was. Well, except when Stan and the boys went to Louisville to that certain bar. Had Nancy known about that? Did she care?

"Well, if she's not on Facebook, where is she?" Don poked at the microwave pancakes on his plate. His lungs were raw this morning, so he'd skipped the coffee shop.

What had George and Jackson talked about without him? They'd probably sat there in helpless silence. Or worse, maybe that new retiree had sidled up to the table, the one who'd started butting into their conversations some mornings. Asking to borrow the paper and then making loud declarations about how much the new jail was going to cost or expounding on the plans to put angled parking spaces on Main Street. George would not be able to resist responding, extolling the virtues of angled parking or recounting how high his property taxes had been compared to Lanier the one year he lived in Chicago.

"You remember the pulmonologist said you should really avoid anything overtaxing until after the transplant." Joyce took his plate and scraped the uneaten pancakes into the trash.

"Running for the school board isn't overtaxing," Don said.

Joyce stood over the sink, washing the plate in the dishwater she would use for the entire day's worth of dishes. Out in Deputy, she'd grown up without city water. They'd drunk rainwater from a cistern filled off the roof, and the whole family lived in perpetual fear of drought and the cistern running dry. The sound of water running still sent Joyce scrambling to find it and turn it off, even after all these years living on city water.

"Well, don't tell the doctor what you're doing," Joyce said. She set the plate in the drainer, her back still turned.

Joyce was convinced that being judged and found worthy was the only way Don was going to get a new lung. That had become clear to him from the first moment the doctor had described the transplant process. He didn't know who she thought was doing this judging. God? The doctors? An anonymous committee that doled out organs on the basis of a complicated demerit system? The details were less important than his growing conviction that Joyce, his own wife, believed that, in the end, he would not make the cut.

Don drew the oxygen tank closer to his chair so he could feel its solid metal against his leg. He banged it against the table as he did, a small reminder to Joyce of his current state of health.

Clank. Waiting for a lung transplant. *Clank.* Barely survived the Covid.

At the sink, Joyce sighed.

"Nancy has lunch at the Main Street Saloon with Liz a lot."

How did she know Nancy's schedule? Don wondered.

Joyce hung the towel on the oven handle and paused with her hand on the door frame. "Don't go on Taco Tuesday, Don. It's so crowded then," she said.

He would go on Taco Tuesday if he wanted to, Don thought.

"Thank you!" he shouted at Joyce, but she was already gone and it was just him and the tank.

>>

Don Blankman was halfway up the stairs when his legs went weak. He'd been sick for days, but he'd kept the scratchy feeling in his throat to himself. He'd gone out in the backyard to cough so Joyce couldn't hear him. When his nose had started running, he'd told her it was allergies. There was always something to be allergic to.

Now when his legs gave up on him, he held onto the railing for dear life, and that was where Joyce found him. Sitting halfway up the stairs from the kitchen, leaning against the wall, one hand clinging to the banister, his lungs on fire. He wanted nothing more than to reach into his chest and pull them out. He wanted to be done with it at last, one way or the other. He held tight to Joyce's arm as she helped him back down.

"We're not going to the emergency room," he gasped out. "I'm not going back in the hospital."

But he ended up there, anyway, pumped full of antibiotics to keep the cold he'd caught from turning into pneumonia, which the doctor told him he would not survive with his bad lung.

"But where'd you get it?" Joyce kept asking. "No one we know has a cold."

What did it matter? Maybe he'd picked it up at the Saloon looking for Nancy, even if he hadn't gone on Taco Tuesday. Maybe at the coffee shop from George, who was probably one of those silent carriers. Maybe Joyce was right and it was just God's judgment on him. He thought he'd lived the best life he could, but what did he know? Everything had gotten so much more complicated than it seemed to have been for his dad's generation. Go to Europe. Kill the Nazis. If it was stressful or traumatic, never bring it up again. Where was *that* America? Where was that silence at the dinner table every night, the quiet dignity of everyone keeping their thoughts to themselves? He could taste the misery in every bland bite of mashed potatoes eaten at his childhood dinner table and there had been no choice but to swallow it down. No one had expected anything else. Why did everyone expect so much from life now? Where had that gotten them? Nowhere but disappointed.

Don had known he couldn't hide his cold forever. Eventually, Joyce would catch on. He knew that, but he had needed those days before the panic set up camp behind her eyes and she'd begun tugging at her hair the way she did, until it stuck up all over her head like a maniac. It was his fault, every time he saw Joyce's hair like that. His failure.

He'd told himself he could will the cold away. Pray the cold away. He had told himself God owed him this, at least. But maybe God didn't owe him anything.

At West Lanier Church, they prayed for him again. Joyce went silent, her hair a spiky mess as she tugged and tugged. "I can't do this," she whispered beside his hospital bed when she thought he was asleep. He was too scared to ask what "this" was.

"I can't do it either," he wanted to whisper back.

>>

Don always woke up when Julie came into his hospital room, like the small space buzzed with an electricity that summoned him back to consciousness.

He wasn't sure if he would see her this time or not. She'd come to check on him every night last year when he was in the Covid ward. He hadn't slept much then either, but they'd slip the stuff into his IV to knock him out.

"I'm so mad at you," she'd said the first night she'd appeared back in June, during his first time in the hospital. She was in her scrubs, even though her shift had ended, with her mask on, of course. She sat in the chair beside him, her head bowed and her hands folded in her lap. "How can you be so fucking stupid, Don?"

"Watch your language there, Julie."

"Oh, fuck off."

He'd laughed. He couldn't help it, even though it hurt. She always made him laugh. Then she laughed, too, and for the first time since he'd gotten sick, he felt like perhaps he was still a human being somewhere under the mask and the plastic to keep in his germs and the lungs that didn't work and the machines that beeped out each moment of his life.

Julie Davis was one of those women who worked even though she didn't have to. Her husband was a dentist who had bought her a mansion on Telegraph Hill, the collection of big old houses that looked down on the river from above. She hated that house, but she'd never told anyone but Don. Julie didn't have to work, but she always

did, even when her children had been babies and she'd run the college clinic and Don was the basketball coach and he watched her for
months in the faculty-staff dining room and in committee meetings
and, God knew, he tried to ignore how he felt. He wasn't a man who
took his marriage vows lightly. He understood he was a sinner, but
he didn't surrender to it. He didn't wallow in it, for Christ's sake. He
tried to ignore the warmth he felt in his stomach every time Julie was
in the same room. He fought it, long and hard. He did.

But then the day came, the two of them alone in the tiny clinic
in the basement of the campus center, when Julie laid her hand on
his arm and smiled up into Don's eyes and he gave in. He could not
refuse that smile. Those eyes. The way they danced with a lightness
Don had never felt but wanted to be next to for a time, at least.

"Well, you're back again, Don." It was the third night of his
second hospital stay when he woke to see Julie's silhouette in the
chair beside his bed.

"It's not the Covid." He tried to sit up straighter, but the movement set off a coughing spell.

"Congratulations." Julie shrugged. He could only see part of her
face, what with the mask, but he could imagine the disappointment
there. "The death certificate will say pneumonia instead of Covid,
when it should read death by stupidity."

"You know they put Covid on all the death certificates, even when
the cause of death is something else altogether. Organ failure and
heart attacks. It's part of the conspiracy—"

"Oh, shut up, Don." She scooted her chair closer and laid her
head on his bed. Not on him, as if he was too frail for that. Maybe he
was. There'd been no sex with Julie or Joyce since the Covid. Joyce
was too afraid she'd kill him. He wasn't sure what Julie's reason was.
Disgust? Rage?

"I'm just saying, if an old bastard like me dies, is it really Covid that killed me?" He picked up one strand of Julie's still-blond hair and let it slide over his fingers. He didn't have much feeling in them anymore, but he still had the memory of how silky and smooth it was, like the pink nightgown she'd worn when they met up at a hotel in Louisville sometimes. "Doesn't seem like it much matters one way or the other."

When he was with Julie, he couldn't stop himself from talking. He couldn't stop himself from saying all the stupid, innocuous things he knew would piss her off and make him look like an idiot, but he didn't care. He would do anything to hear her voice. To know her focus was on him. Just to be reassured that she was still there, even if her annoyance was all he could have. He'd take it. Every time, he would take it.

"You don't have to tell anyone, you know," she said. "Get the shot in secret. Go to another town. No one has to know, you dumbass." Her voice was muffled against the bed.

"What would I tell Joyce?"

"Do you think I care?"

They sat in silence, listening to the beeping of all his devices. The sound of footsteps passing in the hall. A moan that rose from another room and then cut off.

"I'm not going to get another lung, am I?" He closed his eyes and tried the deep breaths the respiratory therapist had taught him. It had always felt a little harder to breathe when he was with Julie. Maybe that was why she'd stayed away.

"Actually, you probably are." She lifted her head and set her chin on her arm, twisting her head to look up at him. "But you shouldn't."

He laughed. "You don't think I'm worthy either."

"None of this had to happen."

He traced a finger down the exposed skin of her forehead to her mask. She had wrinkles, yes, but she was still as gorgeous as ever. Julie Hoss, before she married the dentist. Homecoming queen. Head cheerleader. For a while in her thirties, she and the dentist had been in a band and she was the lead singer, standing on stages in dive bars belting out Emmylou Harris songs in a voice that broke Don's heart.

She'd never said she loved him, though he'd whispered the words into every inch of her body. Against her stomach and the back of her knee and the nape of her neck.

"Julie, Julie, Julie," he whispered. His hand fell away from her face and the next thing he knew, the nurse was coming in to check his pulse and the chair was empty.

>>

"Let's have dinner at the Riverboat tonight," Joyce said.

Don sat in his recliner in the living room, looking out at the river sparkling far below and stewing about Nancy, whose endorsement he still didn't have.

"That's *like* being at the beach," Joyce said.

"It's nothing like the beach," Don grumbled.

The antibiotics had worked or God had decided he didn't want Don yet or for no reason that made the least bit of sense at all, Don's pneumonia went away. He left the hospital again on a Saturday. He'd been in the hospital eleven days and now their yearly trip to Fort Myers was off. Joyce said they couldn't risk it.

"The doctors said to stay close." Joyce waved one of the pamphlets on transplants at him. She kept them all in a neat, rubber-banded stack in a kitchen drawer. She'd studied them closely, underlining the parts she thought were important. "If you're in Florida and we get the call, you'd be out of luck."

"Do either of us really believe I'm ever going to get the call?" he wanted to say, but he agreed to the Riverboat anyway.

They rode the golf cart they'd bought for the grandkids right before he got the Covid. Now it was how Don got everywhere because he didn't have enough breath to walk.

He rolled his oxygen tank down the ramp that went from the shore onto the Riverboat, a restaurant on a boat that floated on the river but never went anywhere, and tried not to think of having to climb back up after they were done. He could hear voices—loud laughter. It was a Thursday night, but the place was packed.

"Is there a band?" Joyce stood at the bottom of the ramp and looked around. They weren't used to places in town being crowded, aside from Taco Tuesday at the Saloon.

Don shrugged and trudged to a table that sat along the railing. A barge had just passed and the whole restaurant rocked in a way that made his legs weak.

"Well, it's nice to see a place doing such good business." Joyce hung her purse on the back of her chair and smiled at the big table where the noise was coming from, even though no one there was paying them the least bit of attention.

Don ordered a beer and ignored the look of disapproval on Joyce's face. If he was going to die, he could damn well have a beer. He picked at the cardboard coaster and stared out at the far shore. He watched the cars, visible through the thinning leaves, crawling up the road out of the river valley. He heard the big table, laughing and shouting, but he tuned it out. Usually, he looked around every place they went in town, doing a mental tally of how many people he knew. Which of them he needed to greet. Which of them he wanted to talk to. There were fewer and fewer people in that category lately.

He was too tired for any of that, so it was only when their fried mushrooms arrived that he looked over at the big table and spotted Nancy.

"I don't know, but is that man sitting with Nancy wearing a dress?" Joyce leaned toward Don and whispered.

He was. A big, hairy man in a sparkly, strapless dress that clung tight to his flat chest. Another man at the table had a feather boa draped around his neck. Nancy was wearing a tiara. So was the man sitting next to her.

"What do you think is happening?" Joyce whispered.

Don shook his head. He had no idea. He recognized Nancy and the guy who ran the new shoe store. That was it. Everyone else at the table was a stranger. Californians, no doubt. They were everywhere now.

The waitress brought a tray of bright blue drinks to Nancy's table and began to pass them out.

"Shots!" the man in the dress called. "Shots all around!"

"Buttery nipples!" someone else at the table yelled, followed by more laughter.

One of the men at the table caught Don's eye and gave a fluttery wave. Don glanced down at his oxygen tank. Still there.

"Is it someone's birthday?" Joyce asked when the waitress brought Don's burger and Joyce's club sandwich.

"No, that's the Rainbow River Club." The waitress smiled and shook her head. "They meet here every month. They're loud, but great tippers."

"The Rainbow River Club." Joyce picked up a French fry but didn't put it in her mouth. She stared at the loud table of laughing people. "Rainbow . . . like?" She frowned up at the waitress.

The waitress glanced over at the table and then back at Joyce. She made her eyes go wide, then leaned down and whispered. "Rainbow like *gay*."

"Oh." Joyce looked at her French fry like she'd forgotten what it was, let alone how it had come to be in her hand.

Don stared at his hamburger. He wasn't going to look over at the table again. God knows what he'd see. He kept his eyes on his plate. Or the river. The river was beautiful. He wasn't going to let those people get in the way of enjoying this meal, even if he could feel his lungs tightening.

"The river's low." He stared at Joyce across the table and willed her to eat her damn French fry and look away from Nancy's table, even as another burst of laughter rolled out over them. "I guess it's been dry."

Joyce tore her gaze away from the table and frowned at Don, like she wasn't sure who he was. "It has been dry."

They talked about the weather and one of the grandsons who'd dropped out of college and how disappointing that was but not surprising. His parents had been so lax with him.

"Did you ever take the survey?" Joyce asked. She was picking at what was left of her club sandwich, pinching off tiny bits of bread, which drove Don crazy.

"No, of course not." Don put a napkin over his hamburger. Looking at it was making him sick. Or was it the rocking?

He'd wanted to take the survey. He'd had every intention of clicking the link and wading into that depravity. Someone had to, after all. Someone had to see what they were up against.

But when he looked again, he hadn't been able to find the email on his phone. It had disappeared. The grandkids told him nothing was ever really deleted, but what did that matter if you didn't know how to find the damn thing? He thought about asking Joyce to forward the email to him, but then he'd have to admit that he was interested.

Joyce stared down at the water. It was a thick, muddy brown, so there wasn't anything for her to see. "I did," she said. "I took it."

Don coughed, in surprise at first, but then because every cough led to more. His body was nothing but an endless supply of coughs. He could feel the big table beside them go quiet as his coughing went on and on. *Mind your own goddamn business*, he thought, but he didn't have the breath to say the words out loud.

"Why?" he asked when he could speak again.

"Why not?" Joyce shrugged. "Maybe it'll help someone."

"How could asking people questions about their sex life possibly help anyone?"

What did it say though? That's what he wanted to ask Joyce. *What questions did it ask? And how did you answer?*

A breeze picked up off the water, blowing his napkin into the river. Joyce watched it sink with an expression on her face that Don could not read. For a moment, there was nothing familiar about Joyce's face, as if while he was in the hospital, a stranger had taken the place of his wife and that stranger was now sitting at his table.

Then her face melted back into the pinched expression that had worn new grooves into her chin in the last year.

"I don't know," Joyce said. "I just did." She put the salt shaker on top of her napkin to keep it from blowing away and turned to watch a barge chug downstream.

"Well, I don't want to hear about it."

"That's just fine, Don." She patted his hand, like he was a child. Like what he thought didn't matter one way or the other anymore.

At the table, a big group stood up to leave and there was a wave of hugging and kissing each other on the cheek, like they were in France or something, instead of Lanier, Indiana.

"Where's the waitress with our damn check?" Don growled.

>>

Joyce had to go to the bathroom before they could leave. She always did, but this time, Don was relieved to find himself alone.

Nancy's table had gone quiet at last. Don allowed himself to glance over. Only Nancy and one man were left. Neither of them was wearing a tiara anymore, thank God.

Don pushed himself out of his chair. He told himself he was sluggish because of the hamburger, but really, he felt like this all the time now. His days had been counted out. Joyce insisted on crossing each square off on their calendar at home, like she was marking time until something, but what? Death. That was all they had left to count down to anymore.

He stood beside Nancy and waited for her to look up. He hadn't seen her in a while, but she was looking good for her eighties. She'd come through the pandemic unchanged. He couldn't bring himself to be the first one to speak.

At last she glanced up at him. "Don Blankman!" She looked down at his oxygen tank. "How've you been?"

Don forced a smile onto his face. Was it not glaringly clear how he'd been? Did she really not know he'd been in the hospital twice now? Did she not know about his lung? Was that possible?

"Just fine." He pulled out the empty chair beside her and sat. He could not stop himself from letting out a sigh of exhaustion, but maybe it would work in his favor. "You know I got the Covid."

"I did hear that." Nancy took a sip of water.

Don waited for more. An expression of sympathy or interest. Nothing.

"Well, I came out the other side all right." He smiled again and glanced at the man across the table. He was somewhere in his thirties or forties. Short and flabby. Too small to ever have made much of a basketball player. The dumpy man rested his chin on his hands. He tilted his head and watched Don.

"That's good, Don," Nancy said. "Good to hear it." She started to turn away from him, back toward the dumpy guy.

"You might have heard I'm running for the school board," Don said.

The dumpy guy raised an eyebrow.

Nancy turned back to Don. "I didn't hear that."

"Schools need some strong moral guidance right now." Don picked up a tiara. "QUEEN" was spelled out in fake diamonds across the front. He frowned and put it back down. "First all the Covid nonsense and now this whole business at the junior high." It was best not to go into specifics. Then Nancy would have to ask or stay in the dark. Either way, it gave him the upper hand.

"Well, good luck." Nancy patted the table and started to turn away again.

"I'd appreciate your endorsement," Don said.

Somewhere upriver, a barge blew its horn. It wasn't foggy, so someone on the shore must have convinced the pilot to give it a toot. Don's youngest grandkid still did that sometimes, waving her arms and pulling her elbow down in the same gesture kids used to get semi drivers to blow their horn. "See me! See me!" Wasn't that what that was all about? Even at that age, kids understood how indifferent the world was. Even then, they sensed how little it would all add up to in the end.

Out of the corner of his eye, Don saw Joyce come back from the bathroom and stand at their empty table for a confused moment. Any minute, she'd spot him and head over. Would she know what Don was doing? Would she ask Nancy about the survey? He didn't know and he was running out of time.

"People respect you, Nancy," Don said. "They listen to you."

She laughed. "That's lovely, Don, but I'm a Democrat. And you're not."

He laughed too and waved his hand in a dismissive gesture. "That doesn't matter in Lanier, does it?"

The smile on Nancy's face froze. She glanced at the dumpy guy across the table, but Don couldn't see the expression she shot him. "Look, Don, I'm not in politics anymore."

"Sure, I'm not asking you to campaign with me or anything. Just an endorsement." He leaned forward in his seat and coughed, an intentional attempt to remind Nancy that he was sick, for God's sake.

But the fake cough turned into a real one and then he had to turn away as the coughs seized his body. Another attempt at expulsion, to get it out of him. That's all a cough was. Trying to get it out, once and for all.

When it was over, he didn't have to pretend to be weak. He stared with longing at his oxygen tank sitting beside him, but he didn't want to use it in front of Nancy and the dumpy guy.

"Don." Joyce's hand came to rest on his shoulder. "Hello, Nancy. Larry."

Don didn't have to turn to see the expression on Joyce's face. He could hear it in her voice. She was angry. Angry that Don was talking to Nancy about her endorsement and angry that she'd had to come over and talk to Nancy herself. Nancy and *Larry*. How did Joyce know dumpy guy's name?

"Joyce." Nancy's eyes flicked to Joyce and then back to Don. Larry nodded. Was he mute? "How are all the grandkids?"

"Good." Joyce didn't go into her usual detailed recital of awards and sports victories and other successes. "All healthy and good." She didn't ask about Nancy's grandkids either. "Don't be too long." She squeezed Don's shoulder and disappeared up the ramp.

Don sagged farther into his chair. Would he be able to get back up? Was a wheelchair next for him? He closed his eyes. "Is there another candidate you're already committed to?" He didn't want to admit that he had no idea who else was running, but maybe that explained Nancy's reluctance.

Larry pushed back his chair and stood. He leaned over to kiss Nancy's cheek. "See you later, lovely." Then he, too, was gone.

Nancy took a deep breath. She turned around in her chair until she could look out at the river. The barge crawled by and Don waited for the rocking to start.

"You're right, Don," Nancy said. "Democrat or Republican didn't used to matter here. But that changed, didn't it? Those days are gone."

"I don't know about that."

"I do." Nancy folded her hands in her lap. "I thought I knew who you were, Don. A good man. Slightly misguided sometimes. A little full of himself. But a good man at the core."

"I am." What did Nancy know? About Julie? The ivermectin? Did she know, like Joyce, that Don would never be worthy? "I still am."

Nancy stared at her hands in her lap. "I can't believe that anymore. I want to, but I can't." Her voice was rough, like every word hurt. "And that makes me so damn sad."

"Nancy." Could he beg her? But why? What would be the point?

"No, Don. I can't do it."

She looked up at him then. Two old people, rocking on a rickety boat in the middle of the Ohio River.

She touched his knee. "I hope you get that lung." She stood and walked up the ramp. She didn't move fast, but her pace was steady. One foot in front of the other until she reached the top. Then she was gone.

Don picked up the tiara. Thought about tossing it in the river. Thought about putting it on.

He unhooked the mask from the tank and took in a deep breath, clean and pure. He imagined himself back in the college gymnasium, the moment he'd known they were going to win the conference tournament. Before he started with Julie. The kids still in the house. Joyce's face still soft and her eyes still bright.

He hauled himself up out of the chair and stood at the bottom of the ramp, contemplating its steepness and the weight of his tank. He calculated the heft of his own tired body and the effort needed to reach solid ground. He took the first step.

He could make it. He was Don Blankman, by God.

Sex or the Weather

Could a town have too many drag shows? Was there a per capita limit and had Lanier reached theirs? The population was a little over twelve thousand, which meant … Rachel couldn't do the math, but, still, it seemed like a lot of drag shows.

The Main Street Saloon, where Rachel tended bar, was packed for this morning's drag brunch, even though this was the third show in town that month. There had been the one at the bed and breakfast across the river. Another at the Blue Door, the event space across the street. Then this one, the first at the Saloon.

Rachel poured her twenty-sixth Bloody Mary of the morning and shoved another celery stick into the glass.

The number of drag shows wasn't the problem, really. It was the Bloody Marys and her aching feet and the fact that she was working on a Sunday, which she'd told Bryan from the get-go she was not going to do. Weekday lunches were all he was ever going to get from her. That was a condition of her employment, because she had better things to do (read frivolous novels and nap), but Bryan had begged and pleaded and then offered to pay her time and a half (Was that legal? Did she care?), so here she was, on Bloody Mary number twenty-six.

On the stage at the other end of the Saloon, one of the drag queens did a headstand, her skirt falling down to reveal panties that were elaborately ruffled in a rainbow design. Where would you even find underwear like that? The crowd cheered and laughed, though given how much vodka they'd consumed, they'd cheer and laugh at anything at this point.

Rachel hated Bloody Marys. She hated the smell that was tomato-adjacent rather than actual tomato. She hated the cloudy thickness of the tomato juice in the glass and the way the pulp settled to the bottom if you didn't stir and stir and stir. No drink should require that much effort and still taste that bad.

She hated everything about Bloody Marys, but they were running a special for the drag brunch and behind her, the ticket machine clacked out yet more orders. At some point, between Bloody Mary numbers eleven and twelve, she'd managed to splash the tomato juice in her hair and now she herself was half Bloody Mary. The smell would never go away.

"A packed house." Rachel's best friend, Liz, squeezed into a spot at the bar between Susan, the Episcopal priest, and Sandy, the high school guidance counselor, and blew Rachel a kiss.

Rachel turned her cheek to catch it. "Please tell me you want a mimosa."

"I want a mimosa," Liz said.

"I love you," Rachel said.

"I know." Liz turned to watch the drag queen, who was attempting splits for her grand finale. "Who knew people would love drag so much?"

"Or Bloody Marys," Rachel said.

The drag queen took a few bows before disappearing into the kitchen and, for a moment, the music stopped.

"So, did you take the survey yet?" Liz's voice was loud and several people along the bar turned to look.

"I have no idea where that email came from." Rachel garnished the mimosa with an orange slice and slid it to Liz. "There's no way I'm filling it out."

The survey was all anyone in Lanier could talk about. "Invitation to Participate: Sexual Practices in a Small Midwestern Town," the subject line read. Who was it from? Had it gone to every single person in Lanier? What did "demisexual" mean? Rachel thought she was up on all the latest identities and categories, but maybe not? There were so many questions and so few answers.

"It was fun though," Liz said.

"Is it supposed to be fun?" Rachel asked.

"Does it matter?"

Rachel ignored the rattle of a new drink ticket printing out behind her. She leaned toward Liz over the bar. Even without the music, there was still the noise of fifty-plus people in varying stages of drunkenness.

"Do you know who the email went to?" Rachel asked.

"Everyone in Lanier." Liz took a sip of mimosa. "Everyone I've talked to."

"Everyone?"

Liz shrugged.

The next drag queen took the stage and the opening chords of an ABBA song blared over the speakers.

Had it gone to Sam, though? Was Rachel's stepdaughter part of the survey? Did some anonymous person now have access to the intimate details of Sam's sex life? These were the questions that would not stop swirling around inside Rachel's head. These were the answers she needed to have.

>>

Thirty-five. Thirty-five Bloody Marys she'd made and it wasn't even noon. Her fingers were pruney with tomato juice. Surely they'd run out of the mix soon and she'd be saved.

She pulled the ticket for five more Bloody Marys for table three and groaned.

"Oh, Rachel, isn't this *wonderful*?"

Rachel didn't have to turn to know that husky whisper of a voice, barely audible above the music blasting through the bar.

"Hey, Pam," Rachel said.

Pam squeezed herself between Liz and Brady, Liz's son. They were both too polite to do anything but shift away. Pam was the kind of person people gave way to.

"It's so great to see everyone *together* again like this, isn't it?" Pam said. "After the *pandemic*." In addition to the whispering, Pam had a tendency to emphasize random words, rasping them out while leaning forward in a way that suggested Rachel should know exactly what Pam was implying. Rachel never did.

"And for a *drag show*, of all things." Pam rattled the ice in her Bloody Mary, which was almost empty. "Did *Sam* come home for this?"

"No, Sam's busy. Got a big project due next week." Rachel had no idea if this was true. She was close to her stepdaughter but not knowing-every-detail-of-her-life close. She was just the right amount of close. But a big project seemed like the sort of thing that might make Pam stop talking and go away.

"Wouldn't *she* love this though?" Pam asked.

"Well, they have drag shows in Bloomington, you know." Rachel paused mid-pour. The bottle of tomato juice was almost empty.

Could this be the last one? She could only pray to the bartender gods.

Was Pam asking about Sam because she was gay? Like it was part of the queer handbook they passed out and meant Sam had to attend all drag shows within a hundred-mile radius? Was that what Pam was getting at?

Rachel stole a glance at Liz. Was she hearing this? Could Liz save her from this conversation? No, Liz was turned to watch a drag queen give the president of the community college a lap dance.

"In Bloomington, of course, but this is *Lanier*," Pam whispered. "Isn't it *wonderful*?"

You said that already, Rachel resisted the urge to say. Pam's eyes were half-closed and Rachel wondered exactly how many Bloody Marys she'd consumed.

"*Wonderful*," Rachel repeated. "So *wonderful*."

Pam nodded and the motion made her stumble, bumping into Joyce Blankman, who apologized as if it were her fault and scurried away.

"I wish Sam could have *seen* it." Pam swayed and pulled the celery stalk out of her glass to take a bite, flinging an ice cube onto the floor in the process. That was a lawsuit waiting to happen.

"Me too." Rachel pulled her mouth into a tight smile before turning to carry the finished Bloody Mary to the end of the bar where the waitress, Shawnee, was waiting.

This was one of the biggest upsides of being a bartender—the built-in excuse to walk away from conversations because people needed their drinks and they needed them now. The next time Rachel looked, Pam had moved on to a conversation with Nancy, and Bryan emerged from the basement with a whole new crate of tomato juice.

"Looks like we're gonna need this," he said.

Rachel watched another ticket come up. All Bloody Marys. "Fuck me," she whispered.

She turned her back on Pam and the drink-ticket machine and Shawnee at the end of the bar waiting for her drinks. She marched past the stage and the bathrooms and the tiny kitchen and out into the back alley, where the air smelled like rotting garbage and, yes, sometimes, urine, but anything was better than breathing in the scent of tomato juice for one minute more.

>>

"I'm too old for this shit," Rachel said.

She sat on an overturned crate behind the Saloon, staring at the backs of the buildings along Main Street. They looked like blocks put together by a drunk, full of odd roof angles and extensions that were impossible to match up to the rest of the building they may or may not have belonged to, but Rachel liked to try.

She listened for someone in the bar calling her name, but so far she could only hear the muted sound of the music. She thought about heading down the alley, past where it crossed West Street and then Mulberry, like a river that would take her right to the back of her own house, but she was too tired.

She sniffed at her hair. It definitely smelled like Bloody Mary mix. Her feet hurt and she could barely move her left pinky. Her back was okay for now because she'd taken ibuprofen that morning, but as soon as it wore off, the dull ache would return.

She should do more yoga. Walk in the mornings. Take the fish oil her chiropractor was always suggesting. Get an occasional massage. There were things she could do to ease the gradual decay that was her late forties, but the thought of it was almost as exhausting as the pain itself. Another demand her body was making on her. Stay thin. Use this cream to avoid wrinkles or stretch marks. Floss every day. No, twice a day. God, she hated flossing. When had taking care of her body become a full-time job? A full-time job was exactly what she'd spent most of her life trying to avoid.

And it was only one o'clock. If she stayed, she'd have a whole other hour left behind the bar. She wasn't sure she could do it.

Inside, the ABBA song ended and the sound of applause drifted into the alley.

What would Charlie be doing now? She thought of their living room, the silence they settled into most weekends, with her on the couch and him in his chair. Both of them reading. No amount of money was worth giving that up.

Rachel knew she had a good life. There was no sense in denying it, especially given the minimal amount of effort she'd expended to get it. She couldn't help but feel sometimes that it was a not a life she deserved. Yes, there had been rough moments parenting Sam, but because she was her stepdaughter, Rachel hadn't even had to go through the pain of giving birth. No sweating and bleeding and screaming for her. To have added Sam and Charlie to her life so easily felt sometimes like she'd gotten away with something.

"Do you think we did okay with Sam?" she'd asked Charlie the other night as they sat on the back porch with their evening cocktails. They'd settled so easily into life as empty nesters. Rachel felt guilty about that sometimes too. "Do you think she's okay?"

"Nothing to do about it now if she isn't," Charlie had said. "But, yes, I do think she's okay. As okay as any of us are."

She should believe him. There was no reason not to. But, dear God, the world. The world was a horrible place. Hadn't the pandemic proved that? It was four years later, but Rachel still flashed back to those days, jarring her out of her body when she least expected it. Back to the moment Sam had gotten sent home from campus. Or the day she'd served Charlie the last beer at the Saloon before all the bars and restaurants shut down, hiding their terror in humor and posting a picture on Instagram of "The Last Beer in Lanier, Indiana." Or rushing to the library before it closed and filling a bag with books, random books, whatever, shoving them off the shelves, just so she would have a lifeline of words to pull her through the coming darkness.

She hadn't lost anyone to the virus. They'd been lucky. They got their vaccines and their boosters. But still, when she thought of those days, it was like a balloon inflated inside her chest and for a few seconds, she could not breathe. She wanted to cry. She wanted to scream and scream until the balloon inside her burst and the world stopped and someone helped her figure out what this feeling was, too large to fit inside her body.

The world was horrible before Covid and it was even worse now. No one could survive unscathed.

Rachel sighed.

"Tell me about it, honey."

One of the drag queens—"Shay D" was stitched across the front of her dress, so Rachel guessed that was her name—leaned against the wall, her wig off, her makeup smeared and running with sweat. She took a long drag on a cigarette and kicked off one of her high heels to rub the arch of her foot.

"Great show!" Rachel pushed the balloon back down inside her and pulled her lips into a wide smile. She always tried to be enthusiastic about performers who came to Lanier. Extra grateful to make up for something she was afraid their town was missing. "Thanks for coming."

"Sure." Shay D pulled at the spandex of her tights. Rachel couldn't tell what the theme of her costume was. Maybe there wasn't one? She didn't know a lot about drag. This was only the second show she'd been to. "I love coming up to places like this. Reminds me of the town where I grew up."

"Oh, yeah?" Rachel asked.

"Morocco, Indiana. Ever heard of it?" Shay D pursed her lips and blew out a thin plume of smoke.

"No."

"Morocco." Shay D laughed. "What a fucking name. Population 700."

"Rachel!" someone yelled from inside the bar. Bryan, maybe? Rachel pulled her legs close to her and bent low over her knees, as if making herself small would hide her.

"Someone looking for you?" Shay D asked.

Rachel waved her hand. "It's nothing."

In the gap between the two buildings, Rachel saw Lanier's sole flock of pigeons wheel through the sky and then disappear. She would stay until Shay D finished her cigarette and then decide what to do. She would figure out whether she could possibly make one more Bloody Mary without throwing up.

"Do you feel you can be open about your sexuality in the place where you grew up?" That was the specific survey question that kept repeating itself in Rachel's head. It was as far as she'd gotten through the survey before she'd had to stop. Push her computer away. Lean over their kitchen table and hold her head in her hands.

What would Sam say? How would she answer that question?

Did it scar you, growing up in a place like Morocco? A place like Lanier? Are you permanently damaged? These were the questions Rachel wanted to ask Shay D.

She worried that people like Pam said stupid things to Sam when she came home from college, but it was more than that. More than the fear that Sam would be yelled at if she held hands with her girlfriend in Lanier. Small towns were supposed to be the perfect place to raise a kid, and as far as Rachel could tell, Sam had been happy. She'd worked at the coffee shop in high school. Washed dishes at the upscale restaurant during the summer. She loved Regatta and the various music festivals. She'd had a solid group of high school friends and they were all still close.

But what had Sam lost by growing up in Lanier? Did Sam feel, like Rachel sometimes did lately, that the walls of the river valley were closing in on her? Before the pandemic, Rachel would walk down the streets of Lanier and feel like bursting into song with joy at living where she did. Now she just felt empty.

Do you hate coming home? Rachel wanted to ask Sam. *Did we fuck up as your parents?* Had anyone given Sam crap about being with a girl? Did her high school teachers know? Her soccer coach? Did Don Blankman, who used to pat Sam on her tiny blond head when he saw her in the coffee shop, think she was less than human now?

Did I fuck up? That was the real question, wasn't it, and it had nothing to do with the survey.

Some afternoons Rachel stood behind the bar, watching the same people rattle the ice in their glasses and juggle their tacos while spilling lettuce and shrimp onto the floor, and she was suffocated by the smallness of it all. The smallness of Pam with her whispery voice and the regulars who all drank Bud Light and the stories she'd heard Liz and her mom tell over and over again. She couldn't breathe for the sameness.

On those days, Rachel wanted to get in her car and start driving. Leave everything behind. She didn't know where she would go. Just not here.

"Was it hard?" Rachel asked. "Growing up in Morocco?"

"Morocco was a trip." Shay D laughed and ran her hand over the skull cap on her head. "The old lady next door bought me my first lipstick. Had my first drag show in my grandma's living room."

"They didn't …" Rachel made a vague gesture with her hand.

"Oh, honey. Aunt Lola had a 'friend' who moved from New York City and they lived together for forty years. Just 'friends,' mind you, but everyone in town knew what happened when the lights went out. Half the men in town belonged to a 'secret' club that traveled to the gay bar in Chicago, once a month, like clockwork. That town was queer as hell." She winked at Rachel. "What town isn't?"

"Have you seen Rachel?" Rachel heard Bryan asking the two guys running the kitchen that morning. The kitchen staff came and went so fast, she had stopped trying to learn their names.

"Nope," one of the guys said.

Rachel scooted her crate to the left so she wouldn't be immediately visible through the door, should Bryan look out. She leaned toward Shay D, her mouth lifted in a half smile. "Sometimes I imagine Midwesterners talking about sex the way they talk about the weather," Rachel said.

Shay D didn't skip a beat. "Any chance of a fuck in the ten-day forecast?"

"Awful lot of orgasms this spring," Rachel said. "Good for the corn."

"We could sure use some oral sex or everything will just dry up and wither away."

Rachel snorted, she laughed so hard at that one.

The opening notes of "YMCA" drifted into the alley. Rachel kicked at a hamburger bun that must have fallen out of one of the trash bags, half picked at by pigeons and rats.

The door burst open and Bryan stepped out. "Oh, sorry," he said when he spotted Shay D. He hadn't seen Rachel and was about to close the door again when she waved at him.

"I'll be back in a minute," Rachel said. "Just needed a break."

Bryan craned his neck to take her in. He opened his mouth and then closed it. "Cool," he said. Then he was gone.

"Good boss," Shay D said.

"Yeah," Rachel agreed.

Shay D took a last, long drag on her cigarette before putting it out against the side of the crate.

"Do you ever go back?" Rachel's voice was a whisper, half hoping that Shay D wouldn't hear her to answer. "To Morocco?"

"Not lately." Shay D rolled the end of the cigarette between her fingers. "No one left there."

"Right," Rachel said. "Of course."

Rachel hated the survey. She was never going to answer it. She didn't want anyone she knew to answer it either. The world was so full of danger and uncertainty. Why invite more into their lives?

At the same time, she hated feeling that way, like everything was cloudy and sinister, too stirred up to make out the faces of the people standing right in front of her.

"I'm up." Shay D picked up a pink wig and pulled it on. "How does it look?"

Rachel tilted her head. "A little crooked?"

Shay D stood up, her feet in heels so high they made Rachel gasp. "That's all right, honey. It's a crooked world, isn't it?"

"Yes," Rachel said. "I guess it is."

>>

Back inside the bar, the crowd had thinned out not at all, even though Rachel could see on one of the big-screen tvs that the Colts game had started. No one noticed. The order tickets behind the bar were long enough to dangle halfway to the floor, despite Bryan's best efforts to keep up.

"You okay?" Bryan lined up the glasses for yet another round of Bloody Marys.

"I'm good." Rachel picked up the vodka and began to pour, assembly-line style.

"Who knew Lanier was so kinky?" the drag queen on the stage purred into the microphone.

Rachel glanced up. Was that Shay D? There was the pink wig, but everything else about her looked different now. Transformed. All the exhaustion from the alley was gone. She was effortless on those high heels, graceful and commanding.

"Do we have one more song in us, my lovelies?" Shay D shouted.

Rachel shoved the celery stalks in one after the other and watched Shawnee carry them off to her tables. The bar was a disaster area. It would take forever to restore it to order for the afternoon shift. She should be wiping it down. Refreshing the garnishes. Making sure they had enough ice.

Instead she leaned her back against the shelves of liquor, pushing at just the right place until her back gave a satisfying pop.

"Thanks for *having* us this morning." Shay D winked and then reached up to adjust one of her boobs.

Rachel pulled at the front of her own bra where it rubbed across her stomach. She couldn't wait to get home and rip it off. She couldn't wait to get home and shower off the smell of Bloody Mary mix. To put on her comfiest clothes and take a long nap on the couch. To escape the constant deluge that was having to be always attuned to the needs of a bar full of people. It made her a good bartender. It made her weary to her core.

"Here's an oldie and goodie from the original diva." Shay D nodded toward the drag queen running their sound, who nodded back and pushed a button.

The opening notes of a Madonna song drifted out over the bar. "Like a Prayer." Rachel smiled. The crowd grew quiet.

Life is a mystery.

Madonna's voice sang out a capella, and Shay D lip-synced along as the crowd watched, their Bloody Marys forgotten for the moment.

It was a strange feature of the Main Street Saloon that there was a stained-glass window high up the side of the wall that faced the alley outside. Why was there a stained-glass window in a bar? No one knew and it had never occurred to Rachel to ask. She didn't notice the window most of the time.

Everyone must stand alone.

But now, as happened from time to time, the light hit the window just right so that it lit up and cast its complicated, geometric pattern directly onto the spot where Shay D stood.

I hear you call my name.

"Do you see that?" Rachel whispered. Liz was still sitting at the bar, but if she heard Rachel, she didn't answer. She was rapt, staring at Shay D, who, if she noticed the light from the window, gave no sign.

Shay D put her palms together as if in prayer, her skin lit with the reds and yellows from the window.

And it feels like home.

Rachel felt the pause in the song, the notes of the organ soaring up toward the high ceilings. A few of the people bowed their heads. Because they were so drunk on Bloody Marys, she told herself, but was that it?

Rachel hadn't been to church in years, not even on Christmas, even though they lived right next door to the Episcopal church, which was beautiful and the most liberal congregation in town. It had been decades since she'd felt like she belonged on a church pew.

Sometimes though, on Christmas Eve, she heard voices floating across the short distance between the church and their house, with that special quality of sound in the stillness and the cold. She and Charlie would curl up on the couch in their kitchen and listen. Sometimes Rachel would tear up with the feeling that she'd lost something, even if she wasn't sure exactly what it was. Charlie never made fun of her for it.

Shay D lifted her hands above her head, eyes directed toward the ceiling or God. The other drag queens joined her, all of their hands lifted in that pause in the song. The light from the window played across Shay D's face. Rachel felt that this could not possibly be happening in Lanier and also that there was absolutely no other place on earth it could happen.

When you call my name, it's like a little prayer.

All at once, the music swelled, filling the space of the bar. The crowd rose up and sang along, the drag queens moving among them like disciples. Everyone's body swayed to the music, the community college president beside the Episcopal priest. Shawnee and Bryan. Liz and Brady. Even Pam, who looked ridiculous, but no one cared. They all looked ridiculous. They were ridiculous together.

"She is the sexiest woman I've ever seen," Liz whispered, her eyes still on Shay D.

"She is," Rachel whispered.

"Let the choir sing!" the room shouted along with Madonna and the drag queen.

Rachel shook her head. She pulled out one final glass and poured herself a Bloody Mary. She took a deep sip as communion. She wished for revelation. She wished for a certainty she wasn't sure she'd ever known. Most of all, she wished Sam was there in the bar with her to see this.

The Eloquence of Hot Dogs

Loretta hit print and sat back with a sigh.

She'd done it. Mission accomplished. She'd solved the problem of the hot dog guy.

The mayor wanted a way to get rid of the wiener vendor once and for all. He'd emailed Loretta's boss demanding an immediate solution. The hot dog guy wasn't on-brand for Lanier and they'd spent a lot of money on the marketing firm to come up with that brand. Hot dog guys weren't a part of it.

Now the problem was solved and all Loretta needed was a cigarette. She deserved a cigarette. She'd earned her cigarette, but, of course, there was no smoking inside the health department where she worked. What kind of example would that set? She could smoke outside as long as she was ten feet away from the building, but people would see her, and it had been suggested that employees of the county health department huddled around the building while they smoked did not make for the best optics.

"Fuck the optics," Loretta mumbled.

She hauled herself out of her chair and shuffled down the hall to wait beside the one printer they all shared, a sad and ancient device that lived in their break room, like one more hulking and resentful employee.

She was still half an hour away from her lunch break, but she could escape by pretending she had an emergency inspection. There wasn't really any such thing as an emergency inspection. Even if a customer at a restaurant found a whole nest of cockroaches tucked under their jumbo-size pork tenderloin sandwich, there were still reams of paperwork to be filled out before Loretta ever showed up. Paperwork that took days if not weeks to process. Still, only her boss knew that, and lucky for Loretta, her boss was at some conference in Indianapolis today.

She grabbed the pages off the printer, warm and pleasing in her hand. She turned the sign on her door to "Out of office," which the boss insisted they all do when they were gone. She shoved the pages into her purse and made a noise that could have passed for a goodbye toward the receptionist out front. Then she got in her car to head home, where she could take off her shoes and her bra and have a cigarette on her couch, where the optics were just fine.

She snapped her seatbelt into place, one in a long list of new rules she'd been forced to surrender to over the course of her life. When she was young, kids roamed free over the landscape of the car interior and eventually curled up in the foot well behind the passenger seat like small animals. Not anymore. That was life. A series of endless surrenders to one change after another.

But not the hot dog guy. Oh, no. This was her victory. Score one for Loretta.

The temperature readings were the key. A stroke of pure bureaucratic brilliance on her part. The specific high-sensitivity type of thermometer required to get those readings was exorbitantly expensive, first off. So the hot dog guy would have to invest in one, and given what he was charging for his hot dogs, it was unlikely he could afford it.

But even if he could, he'd have to take the temperature of the hot dogs in his cart every hour on the hour, recording each reading carefully on a form Loretta had designed expressly for this purpose. This sheet would have to be turned in to her daily.

She tapped her fingers across the steering wheel. Was that enough? Would it satisfy her boss and the mayor who wanted the hot dog situation taken care of ASAP? Should she make it twice daily, instead? If once daily didn't drive him out of business, she could go for two. It would work. She was sure.

>>

Loretta didn't know the hot dog guy, though his name was etched onto her brain now. Dan Fortlow. Daniel West Fortlow. He'd filled out his full name on all the health department paperwork in his initial vendor application. She knew his address, a split-level on the Hilltop in one of the subdivisions next to the Catholic school. She'd kissed Carly Chandler in the house next door to his during her junior year of high school, just on a lark. Carly was a horrible kisser and did not take direction well. Now Carly was a secretary out at the college and the mother of four. Loretta hoped for her husband's sake that Carly's skills had developed along the way. Or maybe her husband didn't care about that sort of thing.

Daniel West Fortlow had no idea that Loretta had kissed Carly in the house next door. He probably had no idea who Carly was, let alone Loretta. He hadn't grown up in Lanier, because if he had, Loretta would have known his name.

What did Daniel West Fortlow look like? She didn't know. Maybe she could invent another form that required a photo or a copy of his driver's license? Would that be an abuse of authority? Did she care?

Loretta had never seen the hot dog guy because she didn't go to the farmer's market, which was when the hot dog guy set up most of the time. She didn't walk around town all the time like Rachel and Liz. She didn't hang out at any of the coffee shops or the bars or go to concerts or movies in the theater where you had to bring your own chair because the old ones had been sent to a special place in Indianapolis to get reupholstered and, years later, had not yet returned.

Loretta didn't do any of those things because every time she left her house, she could not ignore all that had already been lost. The Corner Market was gone. Some former local news anchor and her B-list reality TV star husband were living in Mr. Knorr's men's clothing store now. Nothing in Lanier was the same, so what did any of it matter? The hot dog guy was just another in a long line of transgressions against the perfect state of the world that had existed in Loretta's childhood, everything since then a slow and inevitable fall from grace as far as Loretta was concerned.

"The mayor has something to prove here," her boss had told her. "That survey has him all stirred up."

The stupid sex survey was all anyone in town wanted to talk about, and for that exact reason, Loretta had nothing to say about it. Sex was sex, another bodily function. What was the big deal?

Loretta unlocked the door to her house, closed her eyes, and breathed in deeply. She'd been trying to smoke less inside, but cigarette was still all she could smell. There was zero hint of the expensive new air freshener she'd plugged in last night. "Spring breeze," the package said, but there was nothing springy or breezy about her house. It was the third air freshener she'd tried, with no success. The house smelled of cigarettes, just like it had when it had been her mother's house and her grandmother's before that.

"Better than smelling like cat pee," Loretta imagined her mother saying.

Cigarette smoke and cats—that would be the brand of the women in Loretta's family, the number of cats increasing through the generations. Grandma Pat had one. Loretta's mom had gotten up to three at one point. Loretta had maxed out at five, just before her mother had died, sixteen years ago now.

Loretta had been mere pages away from finishing her dissertation when her mom had gotten sick. She was getting a PhD in folklore, which her mom was convinced was something Loretta had made up. She would have majored in witchcraft if there had been such a thing, but there wasn't. Folklore was as close as Loretta could get. Witchcraft was her specialty, at least.

Loretta had been deep in the research for her dissertation, exploring the herb lore of Irish midwives in the nineteenth century. She'd dreamed in potions and poultices. She had been so close to being done and she'd had no idea what would come next, but it would not involve going back to Lanier.

Then her mother had found the lump and Loretta was an only child. There was no one else to take care of her. Loretta had packed up three boxes of her belongings, most of them copies of microfiche documents from Irish women's diaries, and driven across the country, back to Lanier.

Her mom was down to no cats when Loretta had arrived. She'd let them die off one by one with no replacement, as if she were determined to sink into complete and utter loneliness. The first of Loretta's cats had appeared while her mom was still in the hospital, an orange tabby that was the ugliest cat Loretta had ever seen. Still, she fed him. He was there waiting when she came home from a long day at the hospital watching her mother show more kindness to the nurses and the doctors than she had ever directed at Loretta. The nurses and doctors loved Loretta's mom. "Aren't you lucky to have her for a mom?" they said to her, their faces lit up, and Loretta nodded. She was. She was lucky. Of course she was.

Loretta picked up the next cat at the animal shelter the week they sent her mother home to die, the two of them alone in the house except for hospice visits that never lasted long enough. Her mom complained about the cats. She didn't want them in the room with her. She'd developed an allergy in her illness, her mother claimed. The cats made her sneeze. They hurt her tender skin when they walked across her body.

But when Loretta stood on the other side of her mother's closed bedroom door, she could hear her whispering to them, sweet nothings about how beautiful and soft they were. She would find them snuggled up with her mother on the bed, her hand still resting on their warm bodies. In those moments, Loretta hated the cats.

Now Gus was the only one of those original cats who was still alive, sixteen years old and feeling every bit of it. Loretta's friend Tom had brought Gus to her as a kitten one month after her mom had died.

"I don't want another cat," Loretta had said. "Get it out of here."

She had been sad, of course. Her mother was dead. She had no idea what would happen next. Feeding the cats was the only thing that got her out of bed. But one day, standing at her kitchen counter with the cats swirling around her legs and waiting for their treats, she realized that she was relieved. She realized that with her mother gone, she could breathe at last. She couldn't say that out loud though. Not even to the cats.

Now Loretta plopped down on the couch, her butt, as always, landing right on the place where the cushions had thinned out and the hardwood frame poked through underneath.

"Dammit all to hell," she said.

She should buy a new couch. She should paint the walls a new color. She should rip up the shag carpet that had been there so long she wasn't even sure what color it had started out as. But she didn't. Everything in the house was exactly the same as it had been when her mother died.

Gus wobbled into the room on unsteady feet. He couldn't reach his back to clean himself anymore so she had to cut the matted fur off every couple of weeks. He'd started peeing in a corner of her bedroom and that meant it was the beginning of the end, but she couldn't put him down, any more than she could buy a new couch.

"Why do you think you won't make your house your own?" This was the question her therapist had asked her. This was the question more than one therapist had asked her. She'd been through three of them, hoping that maybe it would help her get her life going again. Every one of them wanted to talk about her mother, but Loretta didn't have anything to say about that. She wasn't one of those people, the kind who blamed all their problems on mommy or daddy issues. The nurses and doctors had been right. Loretta was lucky to have her mother and that was that. Nothing more to say.

Gus stopped his unsteady weave to stare at her.

"No one asked you, Gus." She unhooked her bra and pulled out a cigarette, trying to recapture that moment of joy at besting the hot dog guy. That was how life was though. The good moments never lasted.

>>

Tom came over on Saturday and insisted that Loretta go for a walk with him, instead of sitting at her kitchen table drinking coffee while she smoked one cigarette after another, which was what they usually did together.

"Getting some air will be good for you," Tom said. He was wearing the bright orange sneakers she'd seen on his feet every time he'd come to visit during the twenty years he lived in New York, and that was some comfort to Loretta. Though if he'd owned the shoes that long, it was fair to say he probably hadn't done that much walking in them.

"Do you know me?" Loretta squinted at him as he stood on her front step, refusing to come in like a normal human and sit down. "Since when have I cared about what's good for me?"

"Well, maybe I care," Tom said. "Anyway, it's all the rage now. No one has coffee or drinks anymore. Everyone goes for walks together instead. Because of Covid, but now, it's multitasking and all."

"I hate it."

"Do it for me and my belly." Tom patted the place where the buttons on his shirt bulged.

"Fine."

Loretta was not going to put on sneakers though. The idea that you'd own a whole separate pair of shoes just for walking was abhorrent. While she was bent over to pull on her garden clogs, Gus slipped out the door.

"You're too old to go out, Gus!" Loretta yelled. "If you get weak and can't make it back home, on your own head it will be."

"Gus is tougher than he looks," Tom said.

Loretta didn't think that was true, but she didn't have the energy to argue. She was already exhausted and they hadn't even started.

"Let's walk down Main Street." Tom waved his hand up the street, like he was Mickey Mouse at Disneyland instead of her best friend inviting her to walk on a street she knew better than the contours of her own face.

"Fine," Loretta said.

This was how Tom was since he'd moved back from New York with his husband. Lanier was like Disneyland to him. Everything was so delightful. Everything was so easy compared to life in a big city. How long before the shine wore off, Loretta wondered. She'd known Tom since they were babies and the one constant in his life was restlessness. He said he was in Lanier for the duration, but Loretta doubted it. He'd go back to New York or California or Prague or whatever new place took his fancy, leaving her alone in Lanier, again.

"Did you take the survey?" Tom asked.

"No," Loretta said.

Tom shrugged. "I didn't think you would."

They turned onto Main Street where the Corner Market used to be. Now it was an upscale home goods store, only everything in there was painted white. White chairs. White planters. White signs that said "JOY" in faded gray letters. People ate it up.

Loretta ran her fingers across the potted rosemary plant, trimmed into a tight ball, that sat outside the store. She raised her hand to her face and inhaled. She didn't have anything to say about the sex survey. She had bigger fish to fry. She'd turned in her proposed regulation for the hot dog guy to her boss on Friday. Would the boss go for it? Loretta had worked harder on those five pages than she had on anything she'd ever done at the health department. She'd worked harder on those five pages than she had since her dissertation. She was proud of them, which was pathetic. She was pathetic. There was something satisfying about admitting it.

"Do you remember that book Cindy gave you?" Tom stopped, waiting for the crosswalk light to change.

"What book?"

"Cindy" was what Tom had always called her mother. Never Mrs. Sawyer. Never "Loretta's mom." Always Cindy. Loretta had tried it once, calling her mother by her first name.

"Who exactly do you think you are?" her mother had said when Loretta attempted it, that tone in her voice that always made Loretta flinch. Not that she thought her mom was going to hit her. She'd been too old by then. But the tone felt the same as one of her mother's slaps, like there was a sore place inside Loretta that only her mother's voice could touch.

"The book about sex," Tom said. "Remember, we used to pull it out from under your bed and look at it over and over again?"

"That book." Loretta peered inside the windows of the dentist's, which was where their elementary school principal had lived and then a lawyer who made the downstairs into his office. "What about that book?"

"Just one of the survey questions made me think of it."

"Hmm." How much farther would Tom expect her to walk? She should have asked. No, she should have imposed some limits. Twenty minutes. And no route that went down to the river, because that would involve going uphill on the way back. Loretta did not go uphill.

"It was this question about how you first learned about sex and did you have sex education, and all I could think of was Cindy and that book and how it just showed up in your room one day." Tom stopped to study a for sale sign in front of the Waxman funeral parlor, the last one left downtown. He was obsessed with real estate. Maybe it was a New York thing.

"It didn't just show up." Loretta wondered if she had enough time while they were stopped to smoke a cigarette. "There was a note inside that said if I had any questions, I should never be afraid to ask her."

"Right." Tom laughed. "Like you were going to do that."

"I could have though." She resisted the urge to groan when Tom started walking again. "It was better than what most parents did though, wasn't it? What did Marge and Gary tell you? Nothing."

"Oh, please, do not make me imagine a sex talk from Marge and Gary." Tom grabbed his stomach and made a gagging noise. "The horror."

"Right, well the book was better than that." Loretta had always thought Tom's mother, Marge, was a beauty. Her memory of Gary was fuzzy. He'd moved to New York when they divorced, taking Tom with him for most of high school, stealing her best friend away. Gary she could take or leave.

"Was it though?" Tom waved at someone across the street. Loretta didn't recognize them. One of Tom's new friends. "All I remember was that it described an orgasm as like a sneeze. Like, *o-kay*? I guess?"

Loretta remembered that too. And the cartoonish drawings of the naked women and men. The women were all fat and the men entirely too hairy. Had she half expected that she would sneeze the first time she had an orgasm? Maybe.

"It was a good book." Loretta stared across the street at the build- ing that had been turned into upscale apartments she could never afford and the soda fountain that was now a pizza place. This was why she didn't go for walks. She knew the town had changed. She didn't need to have it flaunted in her face. "I would've given it to my kid."

"Sure," Tom said.

"I'm going home." Loretta stopped short in the street. Fuck this walk.

"You don't want to see where they're putting in the new brewery?"

"I do not." She could feel where her clogs had already rubbed the back of her ankles raw, the pain a satisfying confirmation of what a bad idea it was to walk. And what would Gus be doing, now? Meowing to get back in. Shivering in his old-cat bones.

"Okay." Tom smoothed his hand over his stomach, which did nothing for the bulging buttons. "I'll see you around."

"Yeah, yeah." Loretta turned off Main Street as soon she could, into one of the alleys, which were the one part of town that remained unchanged.

>>

"So that's all sorted, then," Loretta said. She shifted around in the low, backless chair in the therapist's office, trying in vain to get comfortable. The therapist—Loretta had forgotten this one's name—tilted her head and watched.

The therapist didn't give a damn that Loretta's chair was uncomfortable. It was intentional, for all Loretta knew. What happened to the couches you always saw on TV and in the movies? Loretta was being cheated out of the comfortable couch every other therapist seemed to have. If there was a comfortable couch here, she could fall asleep on it. Who would stop her? It was "her time." That's what the therapists were always telling her.

"Good," the therapist said. This one was young and one half of her hair was shaved, the other half long.

Loretta had just finished telling her the saga of the hot dog guy. She could talk about that for hours and she always struggled to fill the pointed silence during therapy. The boss was running her proposal by the county lawyer, but Loretta was optimistic. Her last thoughts as she drifted off to sleep at night were to imagine the hot dog guy's face as she informed him of the new regulations. Technically, it would probably not be Loretta who would tell the hot dog guy, but in her fantasy, it was.

"What else is going on?" the therapist asked.

Loretta tried crossing her legs, but that didn't help. The chair really was horrible. "I had this stupid conversation with Tom the other day."

"Tom is …?"

"A friend." Her best friend, but she was too old to call him that.

"What did you and Tom talk about?" the therapist asked.

"This book my mom gave me when I was little," Loretta said. "A sex book."

The therapist raised one eyebrow and waited.

"You know, a book that explained the facts of life." Loretta shrugged and let her eyes roam around the room, looking at anything but the face of the therapist. She wished there were a window. A window gave you a legitimate place to look. How long could she reasonably stare at a painting of clouds though? Not long enough. "I thought it was a good idea, that Mom gave me that book. I mean, a lot of other parents didn't say anything. And it's not like there was any sex education in school back then. I mean, there probably isn't now either. But, then? I think we watched some video about periods and body odor and that was it."

The therapist's head moved in the tiniest of nods.

"So, I felt like Mom was ahead of the game, but Tom didn't think so. I don't know. He was awfully interested in the book at the time." She pictured Tom, sitting on her bedroom floor, flipping through the pages of the book and drinking root beer, which her mother had bought just for him. Mom had loved Tom. She bought his favorite root beer and barbecue chips, the smell of which made Loretta gag, but no one cared. Her mom said more than once that Loretta could do worse than to marry Tom. That was before she knew he was gay.

"Of course, the book didn't say anything about gay sex," Loretta added.

"You don't talk about your mom much," the therapist said.

Oh, here we go. "She was a good mom," Loretta said. "I had a good childhood. It couldn't have been easy for her, being a single mother."

"And you gave up grad school to take care of her, right?" The therapist flipped through her notes.

Loretta forgot she'd told this one about that. In the intake session. She'd talked to so many therapists, it was hard to keep track of what she'd told to who.

"Yeah, I had to." Loretta wondered if the therapist would care if she sat on the floor. It had to be better than the chair. Maybe she could lie down. Take a nap. That would be a more productive use of her time than this.

"That must have been hard though," the therapist said.

Loretta shrugged. When her mother had been sick at the end and it was just the two of them, Loretta realized how finely attuned she was to the way her mother's emotions sequenced, over and over again. Panic first. Her mother hadn't been ready to die. She hadn't said it, but Loretta knew. That stuff people said about mothers and daughters—it was true. She could feel what her mother felt. She'd always been able to, whether she wanted to or not, so she knew her mother was panicked.

She'd reach out to comfort her mom. To touch her hand or smooth her hair. "I know it's hard," she had said to her once.

Then like a switch had been flipped, the panic disappeared, replaced by rage. "It's not hard," her mother had said, her voice sharp. "Why would you say that?"

"I don't know, Mom! Maybe because you're dying!" That was what Loretta wanted to say, but she didn't. She had been too scared to talk back to her mother, even in her forties.

Her mom's rage had flared hot for a moment and then it faded to silence, a simmering under the surface. Was that better or worse? Loretta had spent a lot of time contemplating that as her mother slept or stared out the window in stony silence. She'd wished for a sibling in those moments, someone else to be on the inside of this with her. She couldn't explain it to anyone else. She'd tried.

"But your mom's so nice," people would say. "So sweet." Even Tom would say that. And it was true. It absolutely was. It was Loretta's mother who took Aunt Gerdie to the grocery when she couldn't drive anymore. It was Loretta's mother who watched her young neighbor's baby sometimes while she ran errands, even if her mother complained and told everyone the woman was really sneaking off to fool around with her ex, who was clearly no good for her.

Everyone loved Mom. And Mom loved Loretta.

"Do you miss her?" the therapist asked. "Your mom?"

"Of course," Loretta said. "Of course I miss her. What kind of daughter wouldn't miss her mother?"

"Lots of kinds," the therapist said.

Well, not Loretta.

>>

Loretta kept going to one therapist after another mostly because it was free. At least five sessions a year were, which was all she was ever going to do, anyway. That was what their health insurance covered or at least that's what Loretta had thought. When she got a bill for the three sessions she'd been to and it was over three hundred dollars, she was understandably enraged. There was no way she was going to pay for therapy that didn't even work.

"What the hell is this?" she emailed the human resources person.

Loretta sat at her desk, refreshing her inbox every minute as she waited for a response. She was so focused on the screen and her rage that she didn't notice her boss until he knocked on the doorframe.

"There's a glitch," the boss said, one foot out of Loretta's office and one foot in, as if he wanted to be ready to flee.

"I know." Loretta gestured at the therapy bill on her desk. "Damn insurance."

"What? No, not that." The boss jangled the keys in his pocket. "The hot dog guy. There's a glitch there."

The county lawyer was worried that the excessive number of temperature readings required by the new regulation might set them up for a harassment suit, the boss explained. Discrimination at the very least.

"Discrimination against hot dog vendors? Are you kidding me?" Loretta said. Her voice was loud enough to make the boss glance nervously out the door.

He laughed and held his hands up as if fending off an attack. "Don't kill the messenger."

"So what now?" Loretta glared at the bill on her desk. "He just goes on selling his hot dogs full of rat hair, unchecked? Putting the public at risk with his mystery meat?"

"I admire your passion, Loretta, but—," the boss started to say.

Passion? Her passion? She didn't give a shit about the hot dog guy. He was just another crappy thing in her crappy job and crappier life. But she'd spent time and effort on that regulation. It had been satisfying to think that now she'd be the one making changes in Lanier. There were no hot dog carts when she was growing up and there would be none now.

Loretta's computer made the swoopy noise that indicated a new email. She leaned forward to read the response from HR.

"It's not dead in the water," the boss was saying. "There just might have to be some tweaks."

"You've got to be kidding me," Loretta grumbled.

The HR person was sorry to inform Loretta that her latest therapist was, in fact, out of network, which was why her fees hadn't been covered. This despite the fact that Loretta had asked the therapist woman explicitly if she was in her network.

"Oh, yes, yes," the therapist had assured her. "Of course."

It was all too much. Loretta crumpled the therapy bill into a tiny ball and slammed it into the trash can beside her desk.

"Fuck this," Loretta said.

"Now, really." The boss took a step backward. "No need for profanity, Loretta."

"Whatever," Loretta mumbled.

That was all on Wednesday, and from there, the rest of the week got worse and worse. Gus threw up twice on the couch and then once across her bedspread. Her drier stopped working, which meant she had to hang the vomit-covered bedspread out in the backyard, where a bird managed to poop on it, so she had to wash it all over again. She tried to call the therapist to talk about the whole insurance situation, but every time she dialed the number, it rang and rang. Loretta remembered there was a receptionist in the building there every now and then, but apparently, she just worked when she felt like it and wouldn't that be nice. Maybe Loretta should work just when she felt like it. How would that be?

She called Tom to complain, but he was at some conference in Florida and didn't have time to talk. When she woke up Saturday morning, Gus wasn't in his usual place at the end of her bed. She had to search the whole house for an hour before she found him curled up on a towel that had fallen behind the couch. When she shook his bag of treats to lure him out, he barely lifted his head. Maybe he was just cold. Or tired. Maybe he was dying. She leaned over the back of the couch, talking to him in her best Gus voice, but his ears barely twitched.

"Fuck it, Gus," she said at last. "You can't leave me now."

He answered with a tiny meow, so weak his voice gave out halfway through.

She sat back on the sofa, the springs poking her in the same place they always did. She picked up her phone to see if she'd missed Tom's call. Nothing. She couldn't stay in the house another minute with Gus dying behind the couch.

She glanced at the time on her phone. Just past nine in the morning. The farmer's market would be open now.

She went upstairs and pulled on the previous day's work clothes. They were clean enough. "Don't die while I'm gone," she called to Gus as she went out the door.

On Main Street, she could see the big flags they put out for the farmer's market from three blocks away. Why did they need flags to tell people there was a farmer's market? You either went because you needed zucchini, or you didn't. When had the farmer's market become a big, fancy tourist attraction, with activities for the kids and a petting zoo and food trucks?

And a hot dog cart. Don't forget the hot dog cart, even if he wasn't officially a part of the farmer's market. Loretta could smell the salty, sharp scent of the hot dogs long before she found the cart. The aroma hit her somewhere beneath her belly button with the memories of backyard barbecues and trips to the ballpark and the beans and weenies that Grandma Pat would make her sometimes when it was just the two of them.

Nostalgic crap. She would not let herself be distracted.

When she spotted it at last, the hot dog cart was smaller than she thought it would be. Really no bigger than a grocery cart. It was yellow and orange, with a cartoon wiener dog painted on the side and a yellow and orange umbrella to match.

She crossed her arms tight across her chest and waited for the woman in front of her, who was buying a hot dog for herself and a little boy who bounced around her with a balloon that kept hitting Loretta in the face.

"Sorry, sorry," the woman repeated.

"It's fine," Loretta said.

The little boy could not decide if he wanted ketchup or mustard or both on his hot dog. "What does it matter?" Loretta wanted to scream at the kid but did not. She used the opportunity instead to study the hot dog guy's face.

Daniel West Fortlow. He was in his forties. Younger than Loretta expected. And thinner. Surely a guy who sold hot dogs should be a little on the chubby side. Dan Fortlow was not. He looked like the unremarkable guy in an '80s cover band, not the singer or the lead guitarist. The bass player who stood at the back, staring at his guitar through the whole set so that no one remembered his face afterward.

"There you go, young man," Dan Fortlow said as he finally handed the kid his hot dog.

He was the kind of guy who called kids "young man." Loretta focused on how annoying this was to distract herself from Dan Fortlow's smile, which, unlike the rest of him, was impossible to forget.

"What can I get for you this fine afternoon?" he asked Loretta when the woman and her son finally moved on.

"You're ruining my life," Loretta said. This was not what she'd rehearsed in her head. It was just what came out.

The smile on Dan Fortlow's face disappeared like it had been wiped clean. He blinked at Loretta. "I'm ruining your life with hot dogs?"

"Yes," Loretta said.

Dan Fortlow frowned. "I didn't know that was possible." He wiped a smear of ketchup off the top of the cart. "I guess you'll have to explain."

"Why are you doing this?" Loretta planted her hands on the top of his cart and then was knocked off balance when it rocked. That had to be a violation of some sort. So unsafe. "No one wants your stupid hot dogs."

Even as she said this, her mouth was watering at the smell wafting out of the cart. She remembered from his application that he made his own pickle relish. Baked his own buns. But that was not important. That was not the point.

Dan Fortlow tilted his head and studied Loretta. "Do *you* want a hot dog?" He flexed one of his hands, which was covered with a clear plastic glove, as per health code regulations. "On the house?"

"No." Loretta glanced toward the farmer's market, where people were standing in little clumps talking to each other. Some of them sat at picnic tables eating their hot dogs. She saw Liz and Charlie at a table with Rachel. Did they have hot dogs? Traitors.

"Okay." Dan Fortlow pursed his lips and stuck his hands in his pockets. "What *do* you want?"

Loretta surveyed the booths and tables of the farmer's market around them. What did she want?

Mom had gone to the farmer's market every Saturday starting in late June, on a quest to get the first tomatoes of the season. Mom had loved tomatoes. She craved them all year round. Every year she'd bought a bag some farmer had sworn up and down were homegrown, but Mom knew they were not. It was too early for homegrown toma-toes. The tomatoes were too pretty. Too mushy. Too tasteless. Mom would spend the next few days railing at the duplicitousness of it all. The betrayal of those first tomatoes seemed to erase all her joy when the truly homegrown tomatoes arrived. Or maybe that was just how Loretta remembered it.

Loretta stared up at the inside of Dan Fortlow's umbrella, glow-ing orange and yellow. It felt warm under there. Safe. Contained.

"I want things to be the way they used to be," Loretta said. She closed her eyes and felt the heat off the cart, trapped under the umbrella. "I'm tired of everything changing all the time."

"Man, oh, man," Dan Fortlow said. "No kidding. Slow down, already. Right?"

Loretta nodded.

She felt so alone all the time. She always had, but since Mom had died, the loneliness was like a pulsing under her skin. It itched. It stung. She wanted it to stop.

She remembered the last picnic she'd been to. Right after she'd come home to Lanier. A church event of some sort. Mom had still been well enough to go, but Loretta had slept in and made Mom late. Which meant they'd arrived on time instead of twenty minutes early, like Mom required.

Loretta had driven them to the church because Mom had been too weak to walk. "I'm sorry, Mom," she'd said in the car.

Nothing. No response. Mom had stared straight ahead, so that all Loretta could see was that familiar profile.

"I love you," Loretta added.

Mom turned her head toward the window, her lips shut tight. Mom didn't speak to Loretta at the picnic. Didn't speak to her again until the next morning, when Loretta came down to find her at the breakfast table, bright and cheery and going on about Susan Black's daughter, who was getting divorced.

Loretta stared at Dan Fortlow. "A hot dog is a simple pleasure," he'd written in his application. "The food of our childhood, easy to eat, cupped snugly in the palm of your hand."

Who could be so fucking eloquent about hot dogs?

"I have chips, too," Dan Fortlow said. He pulled a big plastic bag of individual chip bags up and shook it like a weird hot dog Santa Claus. "I like the maple barbecue flavor."

"Yes, please," Loretta whispered. "And a hot dog. Extra ketchup."

Ava and the Pink Lady

Even before the Pink Lady, nothing about Ava's visit to Lanier was going the way Sam hoped it would. Her girlfriend was supposed to fall in love with Sam's hometown. Instead, Ava complained.

Ava didn't want to walk because it was *so hot* down here, like they were in Mississippi, instead of southern Indiana. Ava would only ride in the golf cart they had borrowed from Sam's mother's boyfriend, Blaine. When the golf cart wasn't available because Blaine was riding his friends around, Ava wouldn't leave the air conditioning.

"Why don't we rent our own golf cart?" Ava lay on Sam's childhood bed at her mom's house, her hair fanned out around her. "A blue one."

"It costs too much," Sam said.

"I'll pay," Ava said.

But we can walk, Sam thought. Walking was the whole point of Lanier. It was what you did. It was what she'd spent most of her childhood doing. Walking to the coffee shop or along the river or back and forth between Mom's house and Dad and Rachel's house.

Ava was impressed by the coffee shop but annoyed that they couldn't eat at the Main Street Saloon, where Sam's stepmom, Rachel, tended bar, because Sam wasn't twenty-one yet. There was a moment Friday night when Sam thought Ava and everyone might go to the bar without her, but Jessie, one of Sam's roommates, who had all come down, too, said that would be too mean.

>>

Sam should have known the visit was doomed. The signs were all there from the beginning.

"Regatta? Like, with sailboats?" Ava had asked when Sam had first invited her back in May to come to Lanier for the race.

"No, that's not—What?" Sam had laughed, she was so certain she knew what a regatta was and was not. "That's not what a regatta is."

Then they looked up "regatta" and Sam had to admit once again that every single thing she'd learned about the world was wrong.

"Well, this is a hydroplane race." Sam pushed away Ava's phone with its pictures of rich people dressed all in white, brightly colored sails in the background. "It's loud. And more fun than that."

"Okay." Ava nodded. "What's a hydroplane?"

How did people not *know* this? Regatta was *famous*. There was a whole movie about it. Dad had been to the premiere. There were no movies about the Indy 500 (were there?), which was all Ava's home-town of Indianapolis had going for it.

"There are rides and food and music," Sam said. "It's a thing. You should come."

Her mom's current boyfriend, Blaine, had a house a block from the river, which meant this year, they could sit on his upstairs porch and watch the race. This was such a big deal, but Ava was clueless. Was this what dating people post–high school was like? Uncrossable chasms between their world and yours? Or was that only if you were from Lanier?

Braxton, Sam's ex-boyfriend, at least knew what Regatta was, even if he was too snobby to go. He knew enough to be a snob about it, which was better than the totally blank look on Ava's face.

"Are there gay people at Regatta?" Ava bit at the corner of her thumb, which meant she was nervous, and that annoyed Sam even more.

"I have to pee." Sam fled to the bathroom and sat on the toilet looking at TikTok until she knew she could go back without crying or yelling and then they didn't talk about it again until June, four weeks before Regatta.

>>

Yes, there were gay people at Regatta. There were gay people every-where. What? Did Ava think gayness was something that drifted in the city air but nowhere else? Or the suburban air, really. Ava wasn't actually from Indianapolis, but one of its snootier suburbs.

Why would there not be gay people at Regatta?

Okay, so Craig and Tom, her dad and Rachel's friends who were gay, didn't go to Regatta. But neither did Dad and Rachel. It had nothing to do with them being gay or not.

Sam went to Regatta. *She* was gay.

"Anna and Victoria and Jessie are coming," Sam informed Ava. They were Sam's roommates, all from the Area, which they couldn't believe Sam didn't know meant the suburbs around Indianapolis. But why not just call it that, then?

"Would we be able to sleep in the same room?" Ava asked.

"Yes, of course," Sam said.

Ava twirled one of her bright red curls around her finger and pursed her lips. "Okay, I'll go."

>>

Ava wanted to get closer to the river before it got shut down for the hydroplane races, but then when they walked down by the water, she said it smelled funny. "Like stale mud," which, yes, it was a river. What did she expect it to smell like?

Ava said it was too far to walk across the bridge to Kentucky for ice cream at the Dairy Queen. And when Sam told her the story about how when she was little, she thought the weird metal thing sticking out of the river with bushes growing on top was a house where people lived, Ava didn't laugh like she was supposed to, the way everyone else did when she told them that story.

"Right, but what is it, then?" Ava frowned. "The thing sticking out of the river?"

"Clearly, not a house," Sam said.

"But, what?"

The rest of that day, Ava asked everyone they met what it was until Blaine informed them it was the remnants of a silo for loading grain onto barges, which didn't sound right to anyone.

"What part of the silo was it?" Ava asked. "And what's a silo?"

Sam had to admit that there were good moments too. Lanier had redeeming qualities, if she could just get Ava to see them. They got tipsy on Dad's gin and tonics one night and caught fireflies in the tiny backyard. They held hands at the Riverboat Inn down on the river, rocking gently every time a barge went by (it still smelled funny, Ava said, but the grease from the frier mostly covered it up). No one gay-bashed them. One old lady even smiled as she walked by their table, which Ava said was because she assumed they were friends or sisters, but what did Ava know?

>>

They were sitting at one of the tables outside the coffee shop, a little hungover and picking at their bagels when Ava saw the Pink Lady, pedaling by on her bike.

Sam didn't notice. The Pink Lady was part of the scenery, taken for granted like a tree or a road sign. The Pink Lady just *was*.

"Oh. My. God. Who is *that*?" Ava had the tiniest bit of cappuccino foam stuck on her lip.

"Who?" Sam squinted her eyes against the sun and studied the street. The excitement in Ava's voice sounded like she'd seen someone famous, which was unlikely in Lanier, but not impossible. A tattoo artist/reality TV star had bought an old mansion along the river down the road and people claimed to have spotted her in Lanier. Was that who Ava had seen?

"She's amaaazzzzing." Ava stood up and craned her neck down the street.

"What are you talking about?" Sam wiped her hand across her face and wished Ava would calm down. She hadn't been this excited about the many very cool things Sam had already shown her. What was so thrilling now?

"The bike! The lady on the bike!" Ava bounced up and down on the balls of her feet.

"What?" Sam shouted loud enough to turn the heads of the people at the next table. Why wasn't Ava hungover? Just a second ago, she'd been hungover. It wasn't fair.

Sam glanced up and down the street. She stared straight at the Pink Lady without even considering that she might be who Ava was talking about.

"Pink! Pink!" Ava pointed at the Pink Lady, who made her slow and steady way down Main Street. The Pink Lady never went fast. "On the pink bike!"

"Oh," Sam said. "Stop pointing, already," she wanted to add. You didn't point at the Pink Lady. It was rude. "That's the Pink Lady," she said. She shrugged and pulled her legs up onto the chair, tucking her chin onto her knee.

"The *what*?" Ava stepped off the curb as she tracked the bike down Main Street, as if she were getting ready to take off, to chase the Pink Lady down the block.

"The Pink Lady." Sam licked some cream cheese off her finger.

Ava collapsed into her chair, out of breath with excitement. She leaned across the table toward Sam. "Is she, like, neurodiverse? Is she on the spectrum?"

Sam squinted at Ava, even though it made her head hurt. "No, she's not autistic."

"Is she wearing a wig?" Ava asked. "Is it like performance art or something? Do people do performance art in Lanier?"

"What?" Sam slammed her feet onto the pavement, rocking her chair back in the process. "No, it's not a wig and she's not an artist." At least as far as Sam knew, she wasn't. What was the matter with Ava this morning? Why was she being so loud and so … stupid? "The Pink Lady just—" Sam searched for the right words but couldn't find them. She'd never thought to explain the Pink Lady before. She didn't require explanation. She simply was. "She just likes to ride her bike a lot."

Ava raised an eyebrow, the beginnings of a smirk pulling at her lips. "Okay." Ava tucked her hair behind her ear. "Got it."

Sam kicked her shoe against the table leg.

Okay, so the Pink Lady did look different. That was true, though most people in Lanier didn't much notice those differences anymore.

It was the Pink Lady's hair, mostly. Long and thin with bangs cut straight across her forehead. The color was dyed, and it did look like it might be a wig and not a very good wig. Her face was wrinkled and she clearly went to one of those tanning beds, making her skin a little orange-ish, though that itself didn't make her that unusual in Lanier. She wore bright blue eye shadow. The Pink Lady definitely could have benefited from a makeup tutorial on YouTube, sure, but that wasn't unusual for Lanier either. Really, it was the combination of all those things, plus the pinkness.

The Pink Lady moved through the world in a cloud of pink. Pink bike. Pink clothing. Often short pink short-shorts. Pink basket on the bike. Pink way she pedaled around town in an endless loop like she had nothing to do and nowhere to be. Down Main Street or Second or Third. By the river, sometimes. Sam didn't know if she had a set route. She'd seen her everywhere. If the weather was warm, the Pink Lady would be out on her bike. That was just a fact of life in Lanier.

"But … so why is she like that?" Ava shoved the rest of the bagel into her mouth and chewed with her cheeks bulging in a way that made Sam turn away. "Is it, like, trauma or something?"

Sam closed her eyes and shook her head. "No. It's just who she is. She's related to my friend, Tom. She's from here. She's not autistic or traumatized. She's just … the Pink Lady."

"That's amazing." Ava spoke even though she was still chewing. "I want to know all about her."

"There's nothing to know," Sam said.

"Is she straight?" Ava asked.

"Yeah, she's married."

"Married? To a dude?"

"Yeah."

"What does he look like?"

"Normal," Sam said. A little overweight with glasses and a beard. They'd been married for as long as Sam could remember.

"Wow. She could have her own reality TV show." Ava stared at Main Street, as if she were seeing it with different eyes. As if at any minute, something new and amazing would happen.

"That would be stupid," Sam mumbled, but she wasn't sure if Ava heard her or not.

>>

The Pink Lady was just the beginning. The floodgates had opened. If Ava was into weird, Lanier had plenty of it to go around.

There was Parrot Guy, who walked around town with a parrot on his shoulder. And, less frequently, a ferret on a leash. And, once, a kitten he just carried in the crook of his arm and let all the kids pet. He lived in an apartment next to the Main Street Saloon.

"Oh, what about the Parliament Funkadelic guy?" Dad asked. "With the purple jacket and the glasses?"

Rachel chuckled. "Right. James Brown guy?"

"More George Clinton guy," Dad said. "Like he's in a '70s funk band."

"Who's George Clinton?" Ava asked. "Or James Brown?"

They were sitting in Dad and Rachel's kitchen, Ava, Sam, and Jessie on the couch. Anna and Victoria on the bar stools beside the island. Dad was making them puttanesca.

"Translation for the youngsters." Dad opened a jar of olives. "The Black man who dresses like Harry Styles."

Rachel smiled and bumped Dad's hip against hers. "His name's Barry. He comes into the Saloon all the time."

"*Was* he in a '70s funk band?" Ava asked.

Rachel pursed her lips and shook her head. "Not that he's told me, but then I didn't ask."

Exactly, Sam wanted to shout. No one cares why Barry dresses like that or why Parrot Guy has a ferret on a leash or why the Pink Lady rides her bike around town all the time.

"It's sort of like a circus, isn't it?" Ava laid her hand on Sam's leg.

Sam stood up. She wanted to shove Ava's hand off her leg, but then everyone would see. She grabbed Jessie's water glass to refill, like that was what she meant to do all along.

"A circus?" Rachel's right eyebrow lifted. It was a look Sam knew well, but Ava didn't. Rachel communicated in the tiniest facial shifts and this one meant "Are you sure you want to go there?"

"Or Disneyland!" Ava nodded at Jessie. "Like a ride at Disneyland."

"Hmm." Rachel touched Sam on her back as she went by, so gently Sam barely felt it.

"Do you think I could meet the Pink Woman?" Ava asked.

Rachel frowned and smiled at the same time. She tilted her head at Sam. "The Pink Woman?"

Sam picked up the bowl of chopped olives. Thought about hurling it across the room. "We saw the Pink Lady yesterday."

"Oh, you mean Shirley?" Dad took the olives out of Sam's hand. "Why would you want to meet her?"

"She's just so interesting, isn't she?" Ava said. "Like that one quirky character in a sitcom about small-town life."

"You're too much, Ava," Victoria said.

"This isn't a TV show," Sam mumbled.

Rachel and Dad glanced at each other.

"Well, right, but it could be," Ava said. She patted the empty spot on the sofa and nodded at Sam, who pretended not to see.

For what felt like a long moment, there was just the clinking of ice in glasses and the soft simmering of the tomato sauce.

Dad tapped his spoon against the pot of boiling water. "Who's excited about the fireworks?"

Ava crossed her slim leg over the other and leaned forward. "Tell me more about Lanier."

>>

They did not tell Ava about Lorn, the fifty-three-year-old newspaper delivery boy who shouted, "It's a beautiful day!" to everyone on the street. Unless it was snowing. Then he yelled, "Fuck this!" in a voice that was equally loud.

They did not tell Ava that the courthouse cupola had caught on fire the same day the restoration work was finally finished and just a week before Lanier's bicentennial celebration. It was funny now, yes, but only in retrospect. And only if you'd been there.

They didn't tell her about the homeless guy who knocked out power to the whole town one day by attacking the transformer on Second Street because he believed it was colluding with his lawyer to send him to jail.

They kept to themselves which couples everyone knew were swingers and which men married to women everyone knew were gay.

They kept all of this to themselves and, for that, Sam was grateful.

>>

The Pink Lady got her hair cut at the same beauty salon as Sam and Rachel, the fancy one on Main Street. Sam had been getting her hair cut there once when she was little while the Pink Lady was in the chair beside her. Sam's hair had been long and she'd hated brushing it. She had hated for anyone else to brush it. She had hated brushing altogether. It was summer and she'd been swimming a lot and she was well aware of the large tangle at the back of her head.

She sat in the chair beside the Pink Lady, who was getting her bangs trimmed by one of the new girls. The familiar hum of gossip would have been comforting, only Sam was dreading the moment when Celia, the hairdresser, would reach the tangled knot at the back of her head. Sam fidgeted in the chair.

"How's your mom, Shirley?" the new girl asked the Pink Lady.

"Pretty much the same," the Pink Lady said.

"What about this hair?" Celia asked. She made eye contact with Sam in the mirror.

Was Celia staring at the snarl at the back of her head? Could she see it? Was that what she was asking about? Was Celia thinking to herself, *What kind of girl lets her hair get like this?*

"Just a trim," Sam said. She lifted her chin. "And you can cut around that snarl in the back. That's just fine."

Celia's eyebrows rose and Sam could see her suppress a smile. She turned to the girl who was cutting the Pink Lady's hair and the two of them shared a look. Sam sank a little lower in her chair. She wanted to disappear.

She felt a light tap on her knee. The Pink Lady leaned over. This close, Sam could see her eyes were a bright, beautiful blue. They glowed against the orangish skin of her face.

"We have to suffer to be beautiful, don't we?" the Pink Lady said.

Sam nodded.

"It hurts sometimes," the Pink Lady said. She turned and studied her face in the mirror. "It sure does."

Sam wasn't going to tell Ava how much better she'd felt after that.

How she'd closed her eyes tight and ignored the tears as Celia worked through the tangle of hair.

>>

Ava didn't have much to say about Regatta. It was definitely noisy. The funnel cakes were good. She saw some older women with short hair who could have passed for sisters but were "awfully dyke-ish." So maybe she and Sam weren't the only gay people there.

They watched the fireworks from Blaine's porch. Ava and Sam decided to sleep there, snuggled in a pile of blankets, listening to the cars and the people headed home in the dark. The ceiling fans moved the hot air around just enough to make it bearable.

"How many people do you think come for this?" Ava wove her fingers through Sam's hair.

"A lot, I guess," Sam said.

Sam waited for Ava to ask another question, about the Pink Lady or something else she'd seen at Regatta, which had no shortage of strange people.

From the street, they heard the sound of shouting. An argument, though it was hard to make out the words. Someone honked their horn. A baby wailed.

The conversations that drifted up to her bedroom were the soundtrack of Sam's childhood, but she saw now that everyone grew up to different music. Songs so familiar and intricate that there was no language to describe them. You hummed the notes and hoped the other person caught the tune. But what if they didn't?

"It's not like a circus." Ava's voice was so low Sam had to lean her head in close to hear. "Or Disneyland. It's just like a place."

Sam frowned. That wasn't right either.

Inside the house, someone turned off the last light. Above the rooftops and the trees, Sam could make out a mist beginning to drift up from the river. It would get damp on the porch, but she didn't want to go inside. Not yet.

"My favorite time in Lanier is after one of the big events is over," Sam said.

Ava turned her head toward Sam. She could feel her warm breath across her face. "Yeah?"

"Yeah. The morning after. You walk along the river and all the food trucks and rides are still there, but it's all quiet. And then people come and start to pack it all up and they're talking about the weekend and, you know, you get to stay." Sam could almost make out the shine of Ava's eyes in the dark. "They go, but you stay."

Ava blinked.

Sam hadn't said it right. She couldn't find the words for the feeling of those mornings. The sense that the town was hers again and always would be. Maybe the words didn't exist.

"I get it." Ava smiled. She touched her forehead to Sam's. "I understand."

She didn't, Sam knew. She couldn't.

Sam closed her eyes and listened to the sound of Ava breathing.

The Pink Lady would get too old to bike anymore. Lorn would die. Mom and Dad and Rachel said they were never going to leave Lanier, but they wouldn't live forever and Sam didn't have any other family in town. Where would home be then?

"I can't believe they shut the river down for the whole day," Ava whispered.

"For three days," Sam said.

"For three days. Everything stops for this."

"Yeah," Sam said. "It does."

A barge sounded its horn on the river as the mist settled in. Sam pressed her body tight against Ava's.

"I'm glad you came," Sam whispered. And she knew it was true.

Heaven's Waiting Room

Nancy hauled her considerable ass up onto her regular bar stool at the Main Street Saloon and sighed, carefully avoiding the image of the elderly woman reflected back to her in the mirror behind the taps.

"I want something new," she said to Rachel, the bartender. "And fancy." Nancy waved her fingers around, as if she were conjuring a drink out of thin air, which was what it felt like you had to do sometimes in Lanier. "What have you got that's fancy and new?"

"Oh." Rachel craned her neck to stare at the TV screen that rotated through the draft beer list. "Everyone's excited about that new IPA."

Nancy squinted at the rows of bottles, ignoring her reflection. "No, not beer. A cocktail."

"I could make you a margarita?"

"Is it a new and fancy margarita?" Nancy asked.

"Maybe?" Rachel said.

Nancy sighed and tapped her manicured nails across the surface of the bar. How many years ago was it they'd resurfaced it, along with all the tables? She thought it couldn't be more than three years, but that probably meant it was more like fifteen.

"Did I tell you I went to Bulgaria once and swam in the Black Sea?" Nancy asked Rachel.

Lately Nancy found herself increasingly lost in the daydream of being thirty-six again, floating in the waters of the Black Sea, wearing the gray, one-piece swimsuit she'd bought at one of the little stores along the streets of Varna. On the hanger in the store, the suit looked like a large, gray sausage wrapping, but maybe the Bulgarians knew something the rest of the world did not because when she put that baby on—whoa, mama!—it was like a magic spell. In that swimsuit, Nancy was 100 percent babe, with her hair newly short and her body, if not recovered from the last baby, at least not immediately broadcasting mother-of-three to the world.

"You have told me that," Rachel said. "Didn't you swim with the president?"

"Exactly," Nancy said. It wasn't the president. It was the prime minister. Or maybe a lesser member of the Bulgarian royalty. The details had grown fuzzy with time, but Nancy found she didn't have the energy to tell the story again, anyway.

Rachel waved at a group of women who came in and settled at one of the tables in the window. "So, a margarita?" she asked.

Nancy studied herself in the mirror, squinting against her near-sightedness. God, her hair looked just awful today, didn't it? At eighty-one, she didn't want to care about those things anymore, but she also didn't want to become one of those old women whose hair looked like it had not seen a brush in months, food falling out of her mouth as she chewed and staring at people like a toddler who hadn't learned any better. She'd seen a woman like that just yesterday at the Mexican restaurant on the Hilltop. Nancy hadn't been able to look away, even though the sight of the woman had made her stomach turn. "That is not me," she'd found herself whispering. "That will never be me." But she was eighty-one years old, so how did she know? She didn't.

Nancy touched a few strands on the top of her head and glanced away from the mirror. "Yeah, fine, a margarita."

>>

Nancy had filled out the sex survey twelve times now, which was probably going to throw off the results, but she didn't care. If there was a way to read the questions without actually taking the survey, she would do that, but she had no idea how to go about it. She could ask one of the grandkids, but that would be weird to admit she was obsessed with a survey about sex.

It was the level of detail in the questions that kept her coming back.

Have you ever achieved orgasm or climax from oral sex (defined as mouth to genital contact)?

At what age did you first experience penetrative sex (a penis penetrating a vagina)?

Have you ever achieved orgasm or climax from penetrative sex alone (a penis penetrating a vagina in the absence of any other genital contact)?

People were so afraid to spell it all out when they talked about sex, everyone assuming that they were on the same page, but Nancy knew that most of the time, they were not. What was sex? How could such a small word describe so many different things? It couldn't. The survey was right. It required sentences and paragraphs. Treatises. Diagrams. She wished they'd included diagrams. A lot of women weren't even sure where their vagina was.

Every time Nancy took the survey, she answered it differently. She picked someone she knew in Lanier and tried to answer the survey from their perspective. If she took the survey enough times, she could embody the whole of the town. She didn't have access to the detailed sexual history of everyone in Lanier, but she thought her best guesses were pretty accurate.

Like Debra, her best friend, dead ten years now, though every time Nancy did the math and came up with that number, she knew it couldn't be right. Ten years without Debra. Fifteen without Stan. Some days she couldn't decide which of them she missed more.

When she took the survey as Debra's ghost, she figured she had about a 90 percent chance of getting her answers right. *Have you ever engaged in anal sex (a penis or other object inserted fully or partially into your anus)?* Well, Nancy could tell some stories there. Debra had zero filters after a good bottle of pinot grigio on her back porch.

Nancy would never sit on her back porch with Debra again and in ten years the pain of that had faded hardly at all. Talking to Debra as if she were still around, which Nancy did often, didn't make it any better. Nancy could fill out the survey as many times as she liked, but Debra and Stan would still be dead.

Her survey game was about the most fun she'd had in a long time and that wasn't surprising. Covid had been a real bummer. A real crimp in her style, not being able to have lunch at the Saloon with Liz every Tuesday or meet Larry for drinks at the Riverboat. It had been lonely, but she had gotten her vaccine and her booster, so by the time she actually did get Covid, it wasn't the worst thing. Like a scary round of the flu. Everyone had rallied around her while she'd been sick. Booze and casseroles appeared on her front porch. She was still making her way through the crate full of her favorite wine from Rachel and Charlie.

It had been no picnic, having Covid, but she'd also never felt more loved. She'd never felt more held. And that was something. That was a rare thing since she'd lost Debra and Stan.

She loved the survey game, but also, after the twelfth time going through the questions, she'd stood up from her kitchen table and sighed.

"Well that was fun while it lasted, Deb," she said. "What now?"

>>

"Wait until I tell Max that I saw the condos without him!" Larry turned in a delighted circle as they stood in front of the building. "He'll be so jealous."

"Terrific," Nancy said. She stared up at the narrow condo in front of her. "So many steps."

"There's probably an elevator though, don't you think?" Larry waved at the realtor, Jenny, as she got out of her car.

"No elevators." Jenny shuffled through her clipboard full of listings and punched in the numbers on the lockbox hanging from the front door. "But quite a view."

Larry raced up the steps, Jenny behind him. Nancy paused at the bottom, gathering her strength.

What was she doing here? Wasting Jenny's time. Yesterday over their afternoon drinks. Larry had picked up one of the free books full of real estate listings and pointed to the condo with his eyes wide. "We have to," he whispered. Nancy couldn't say no to Larry, and the survey had ceased to entertain her, so she'd called Jenny and asked for a showing.

She lifted one foot onto the first stair. Were they unusually steep? That was a deal-breaker, already.

She was entirely too old to feel this restless. At eighty-one, she was supposed to be at peace. Cruising toward an easy death, hopefully with a nice glass of bourbon at her bedside and chilled out from one of Larry's pot gummies. Liz would be there and maybe Larry too. Not the boys and the grandkids though. She loved them, but they would just be too much while she was getting ready to take the Last Big Step.

That was what Stan had called it. "Nan, I'm almost ready to take the Last Big Step." Then he'd do a quick spin, like he was one of the

Pips, backing up Gladys Knight. His Motown spin, he'd called it. He ended it with a wink and then gathered Nancy into his arms to dance around the kitchen. There was no doubt that Stan's Last Big Step was a dance move.

"I can't even manage *this* big step, Stan," Nancy grumbled. She got a good grip on the banister and began the slow task of hauling herself up.

The condo might have a great view of the river, but the houses on the other side of the street no longer did. Their view had disappeared brick by brick as each condo went up. Nancy's Aunt Dora had lived in one of those houses. Aunt Dora hadn't lived long enough to see the condos built or she would have given the new Dr. Harvey what for. Nancy smiled at the thought. She missed that generation. She'd become that generation, though a watered-down version, all considered.

The condos by the river had been built by the new Dr. Harvey, not the old one. The old Dr. Harvey had died at least ten years ago, but his place in the social fabric of Lanier had not faded with his demise. To make matters even more confusing, the new Dr. Harvey was not the old Dr. Harvey's son but a totally unrelated doctor who just happened to have the same last name. It was confusing and understandably frustrating to the new Dr. Harvey, who had lived in Lanier for thirteen years now, to always be referred to as the *new* Dr. Harvey. And not just forever labeled the new Dr. Harvey but also to have to suffer endless comparisons to the dead man, who was no relation and who had practiced general medicine, as opposed to the new Dr. Harvey, who was a urologist, making very good money off the aging prostates of Lanier. But his specialty didn't matter to the residents of Lanier, to whom he would always be the new and, by implication, lesser Dr. Harvey.

Maybe it was that lingering bitterness that led the new Dr. Harvey to buy the block of empty land by the river and construct a row of four condos to sell that, for the last six years, had become a perpetual source of gossip and outrage.

The condos weren't as hideous as people made them out to be. They were assembled with a tasteful combination of gray stone, exposed wood siding, and glass windows. They would look just fine in a big city block, but in downtown Lanier, they stuck out like sore thumbs, suggesting ever so gently that the new Dr. Harvey knew things about architecture that the rest of the town did not. Was the new Dr. Harvey *trying* to be different? Was he *flaunting* his difference? Did the new Dr. Harvey care about people like Aunt Dora, who'd lost their view? The old Dr. Harvey never would have done such a thing.

All the good people of Lanier had sworn the condos would never sell. Three of them were now on the market for close to a million, which was well out of Nancy's price range, but what else did she have to do?

She paused halfway up the steps and studied the mix of stone and wood. It had a certain appeal. She thought she'd caught a sign of movement out of the corner of her eye in the condo next door as she battled up the rest of the way, but when she stopped and squinted in that direction, she saw only silvery clouds reflected in the windows.

"Are you going to make it, lady?" Larry called from where he stood in the door.

"Oh, shut up," Nancy said.

"It's all open plan, you can see," Jenny was saying when Nancy at last made it through the door. "To take best advantage of the view."

Nancy put one hand against the wall and waited for her bad knee to stop shaking while she took in the condo. The room was full of light, the whole wall that faced the river made up of windows. There were stairs that led up to a second level. A big open room beside a smaller kitchen. Cathedral ceilings. It felt nothing like her shotgun. Nothing like the old Federal she and Stan had lived in on Third Street. The room was too big for her, but she could imagine the appeal—to live with all that light.

"Granite countertops?" Larry ran his hand over the mottled-gray surface.

"Yes." Jenny began reading the details off the listing. "Two full baths. Two bedrooms. Three, if you count the little room upstairs. That could also be used as an office. Jacuzzi-style bathtub in the master bath."

"Jacuuuuzzzi." Larry widened his eyes at Nancy and followed Jenny up the stairs. He didn't bother to ask if Nancy was coming.

>>

Nancy stood in the big room looking out at the river, the sound of Larry and Jenny echoing down the stairs. She drifted toward the windows and the balcony, spreading her arms out in the open space, stretching into all that light.

Every space looked pure when it was empty, before it was ruined by the presence of all the possessions that passed for a life. The couch with the coffee stains and the print from that museum that had faded in the sun from bright yellow to off-white. Moving into a place destroyed that blankness. The light was interrupted. A clean slate ruined. The fall from grace that was the first word on a blank page.

Maybe that was all death was—a big emptying. A return to the potential that was nothingness. That wouldn't be so bad.

Nancy pushed through the door out onto the balcony. She wasn't going to jump or anything. She wasn't that dramatic. She could still hear Larry in the room above, exclaiming over the jacuzzi. He was loud. She liked that about him.

Outside, the wind pushed against the door as she opened it. The river was punctuated by choppy waves, like an expression of its deep longing to become the ocean. Her hair went to hell as soon as she stepped out the door. When she was younger, it had been long and who cared if the wind blew it all around. It was sexy, in fact, like she was a model in one of those commercials. Now the wind just made her hair look demented.

She watched a large bird take flight from the shore. She was trying to figure out if it was the bald eagle that flew across the river and then back up toward the hill every morning when she noticed motion on the balcony beside her. Of course, she couldn't be alone while she was feeling maudlin. There had to be someone to witness her every emotion, didn't there? That was Lanier.

She whipped around to confront whoever it was. That was the sort of mood she was in. She had no patience for bullshit—her own or anyone else's.

"What?" she barked.

On the balcony beside her a man stood holding a watering can. He'd clearly been bent over his very lovely rosemary plant when Nancy had yelled at him. Now he startled and grabbed at his lower back in a motion that was deeply familiar. The watering can tilted and spilled its contents across the surface of his deck and the beautiful outdoor rug.

"Oh, I'm sorry." Nancy walked across the balcony, as if to help him, but, of course, she couldn't, because he was on his balcony and she was on hers. "You scared me," she said, which was total bullshit.

The man pushed against his lower back and slowly straightened. He was older, with graying hair that was thinning a bit, wearing a light cardigan that she thought might just be cashmere, and corduroy pants. That was why Nancy didn't recognize him at first. She'd only ever seen him in his doctor's coat, suit and tie. Even then, it was only ever at a distance and often with a surgical mask hiding half his face. Had he lost weight, too? Was he sick? Was that why she hadn't realized it was the new Dr. Harvey? Had she known he lived in one of the condos? Was that common knowledge she should have had?

"My apologies." He turned slowly and rested one hand on the railing before looking up at Nancy. "Hello," he said.

"I love it!" Nancy heard Larry call from somewhere upstairs and she wondered idly what it was he loved.

She rested her hand on the balcony, suddenly a little unsteady on her feet under the gaze of the new Dr. Harvey in his forest green cardigan that—she could see this well, at least, even without her glasses—perfectly brought out the color of his eyes. It didn't seem right that a man that age would have eyes that green. It made her a little mad and maybe that was why her heart sped up. Or maybe she was having a stroke. She thought about rolling her tongue, which was how you were supposed to tell if you were stroking out, but that would look strange, wouldn't it? On the other hand, he was a doctor, so maybe he would understand.

She stifled a laugh and pressed her hand against her heart, which was going nuts inside her rib cage. Dear God, she was going to swoon.

"Hello." She reached up to pat her hair, but it was pointless. The wind would have its way.

Hot damn, the new Dr. Harvey was a dreamboat. How had she not realized this? Why hadn't anyone told her? Had they all been too distracted with the endless comparisons to the old Dr. Harvey, whose face had always had the appearance of a dissatisfied toad? Or had they all been too angry about the new Dr. Harvey's monstrosities along the river? *This* monstrosity. This monstrosity whose balcony she was standing on beside the new Dr. Harvey, about to pass out from lust.

What was his first name? Someone had to have told her at some point. Bob? No, surely not. She hoped not. Bob was such a stupid name. She'd never known a Bob she'd liked and she wanted to like this man.

"You're looking at the condo?" The new Dr. Harvey was smiling at her. What a smile. No man that old should have teeth that white.

"Oh, no," Nancy said. "Or yes. Well, not really."

He raised his eyebrows, still smiling. What did the grandkids say? Nancy *could not* with that smile.

"I'm in a little shotgun on Third Street," Nancy said. Why was she telling him where she lived? Was she hoping he'd come over? "I just, you know, wanted to see what it looked like inside."

His eyebrows remained in that upward lift.

"Yes, I guess I'm one of those people who looks at houses they have no intention of buying now," Nancy said. "That's me." She tried to shrug it off and felt ridiculous. She was ridiculous.

"I wouldn't mind having you for a neighbor," the new Dr. Harvey said.

Nancy snorted. Was he flirting with her? Seriously?

His narrow shoulders lifted and fell. He had a Mr. Rogers vibe going on and Nancy was surprised by how much she liked it. She glanced at his feet and, sure enough, he was wearing slippers. Nice slippers, but slippers all the same.

Was he single? He had to be single to be flirting with her like this, right? Why hadn't she paid attention to these details? What was the use of Lanier gossip if not to tell her whether this man was available?

"Oh, there she is!" She glanced at the balcony door behind her and saw Larry inside, crossing the big empty room toward her. She was running out of time.

"I'm not sure the neighbors would want me here," Nancy said. She tossed her head, like she was still thirty, with long curly hair that bounced with each tiny nod, instead of the thinning gray mess that was currently standing up all over her head. "I'm a lifelong East-sider. We have a bit of a reputation." She smirked, just in case he had any doubt about what sort of reputation East-siders had.

He touched one finger to the end of the watering can, maybe because it was dripping or maybe because it was ever so slightly suggestive. "Oh, I think you'd fit right in," he said. Then he winked.

"Nancy! It's like a hurricane out here! What are you doing, you old bat!" Larry burst through the door and tucked his arm through Nancy's, pulling her close against him. "Oh, look, is that Rachel walking down by the river? Do you think she could hear us if we yelled?"

"Maybe?" Nancy glanced over to find the balcony beside them empty now. The new Dr. Harvey had slipped inside before Larry could see him. Was that by design? She didn't know, but she was grateful. She didn't want to share this moment with Larry. It was all hers.

"What do you think?" Larry turned back around to face the building behind them. "Are you ready for condo living?"

Nancy smiled and patted one finger against her lips. "It's a more appealing prospect than I initially imagined."

>>

For the next three days, Nancy woke up every morning the same as she always did. She took a quick inventory of what hurt. She noted whether any of the pains were new or particularly acute.

Whether any of her bodily sensations required further attention or concern.

But then somewhere in the middle of this ritual checklist, she'd remember her encounter with the new Dr. Harvey and she'd feel a tingling. Not the alarming kind that meant some part of her body had fallen asleep and might never wake up again. No, this was a different sort of tingle altogether. This, she remembered, was excitement.

"Deb, I flirted with a man." Nancy spoke to her empty kitchen. "And he might have flirted back. Imagine that, can you?"

When was the last time that had happened? Was it when Stan was alive? Stan had flirted with her all the time, which was hard to believe given they'd been married for forty-seven years. But he had managed it.

"You've been married that long, the flirting is all an act," Debra had declared once. "Flirting has an expiration date and yours and Stan's has long since passed."

Nancy hadn't argued with her. It didn't matter. Maybe Stan's flirting had been an act. A well-orchestrated performance for her benefit. That would have been disappointing to a lot of women, but Nancy thought of it only as another sign of Stan's steady love. Love required all kinds of performances. The performance of interest at hearing a story told for the fiftieth time. The performance of joy at getting a frying pan for Christmas. The performance of desire when all you could really think about was the leaky faucet and the kids' lunch and how they would get Liz to her basketball game all the way in Indy this weekend. Performances took effort. Performances *were* love.

That was what Stan's flirting had been and he'd been good at it. She would have given anything to be able to flirt with Stan again. But that wasn't on the table. He certainly wouldn't mind her flirting with someone else, even the new Dr. Harvey.

For the first few days, the tingling sensation and the memory of her conversation with the new Dr. Harvey on the balcony were enough. She replayed that final wink over and over in her mind. She didn't even think about the survey, let alone take it again. Jenny texted her about more properties to look at, but Nancy passed. She sat in the chair in her front room, looking out at Third Street and daydreaming. Which was more than enough, she told herself. It had been fun to flirt with the new Dr. Harvey. But that was as far as it would go. She was old. He was old, too, though maybe not as old as her. Romance at her age was scandalous. Comical.

It wasn't like she was going to bump into him, anyway. Her regular social circles didn't intersect with his. She'd never seen him anywhere but at the hospital. He didn't go to the Main Street Saloon, where Nancy had lunch with Liz at least twice a week. She'd definitely never seen him at the Rainbow River Club, which she went to with Larry once a month, a gathering of all the gay and "otherwise creative" people in town, as Larry liked to say.

So where did the new Dr. Harvey hang out? she wondered. Was he one of the pickleball crowd? She knew *about* this intense social circle, though none of her friends were in it. Too competitive. She'd been sporty when she was young. Now it would just get in the way of cocktail hour.

The pickleball crowd intersected with the volunteer crowd and the churchy crowd, the old folks who spent all their free time giving away food or teaching people how to read. Nancy had great admiration for that but not much patience.

Was there a whole other crowd of retired doctors that she didn't know about? Or was the new Dr. Harvey a recluse, moving in none of the accepted social circles for the old and retired in Lanier? Nancy wasn't sure if that made him more or less appealing. Maybe he didn't have time for the social life of Lanier because he spent all his time traveling, doing those riverboat cruises of Europe and Asia. Men could do those sorts of things by themselves. He'd be seen as a brave and tragic figure, the lone single man of a certain age in every group. Nancy would be seen as pathetic if she did that sort of trip alone. Some things didn't change no matter how old you got.

The social life of the new Dr. Harvey didn't matter though. She would milk the thrill of their encounter for the next week or so. Then she'd go back to the old comforts, even if they weren't as comforting as they used to be. She had no right to be discontented, as good as her life had been.

She remembered seeing a brochure once that had described St. Petersburg (the one in Florida) as heaven's waiting room, because of all the retirees. She didn't know about heaven and all that, but the metaphor worked. That's where she was living now. In heaven's waiting room, and there was very little flirting there. There certainly weren't any new romances. No, in heaven's waiting room, you sat quietly and read the magazines. It was a little boring, yes, but there was no sense in complaining.

That's what she told herself a week later as she sat at one of the long tables in the window of the Main Street Saloon. She'd given up on a new cocktail or a margarita and settled for her favorite bourbon. The table she sat at was reserved for parties of four or more, but that afternoon, Nancy didn't care about the rules. She could be a little saucy. That was still allowed.

Anyway, chances were someone would join her and Liz at their table and they'd end up as a party of four. It was just too beautiful a day for her to sit at the bar, where the light was muted and the wood finish was faded and nicked, even if she still thought of it as new. At this table, there were windows on two sides, so it was like sitting inside a sunny fishbowl, watching people pass by on the street outside.

Nancy held her bourbon up to the sunlight and watched the pattern it cast across the table, like topaz and amber gemstones. It was beautiful. It was enough. There was still pleasure to be had here at the end.

Carole King's voice came over the speakers. What song was it? Nancy jiggled her bum knee and hoped that she'd be able to get back down off the high stool if she needed to pee, which inevitably she would.

"And it's too late, baby, now it's too late," Carole King's voice sang. Nancy laid her wrinkled fingers flat across the tabletop, the orange light from the bourbon glass bright against her skin.

Suddenly, she was back on that bus, being driven to the Black Sea in her gray swimsuit. The radio had been playing this song. Or maybe not this one specifically, but something by Carole King, whose voice always sounded like she'd just finished crying for three hours straight.

"You will be amazed," the Bulgarian tour guide had said. Her trip had been part of an exchange organized by the state government. For local officials to learn about education systems in their "sister city" and spread the good news of democracy around the world. Nancy had only cared that it was paid for and none of her children would be coming with her.

"The Black Sea. Such a vision. You will never forget." The tour guide had flirted with Nancy mercilessly, once growing so brave as to pull one of the curls in her hair straight and watch it spring back into shape. Nancy had indulged him, like a queen. Like the Queen of the Black Sea.

And he had been right. Here she was, sitting in a bar in Lanier,

Indiana, almost fifty years later, and that vision of the Black Sea was still as clear to her as if it had happened yesterday.

She blinked and felt a coolness travel down her face. What new sensation was this? But when she raised her hand, she found it was just a tear.

"Look at me, Deb," Nancy whispered. "Crying in the damn Main Street Saloon. This is what it's come to."

She held her phone in front of her, trying to remember how to reverse the camera like Liz had showed her, so she could check her makeup. Someone knocked on the glass window in front of her. She waved without looking up from her phone. No doubt it was Liz. Or one of the other lunch regulars. If her mascara had smeared, she'd have to get up off the damn stool and go to the bathroom. Or maybe she could fix it with a napkin, if she could get the damn camera to turn around.

"An East-sider in a bar before noon." The new Dr. Harvey stood at the end of the table, a smirk on his face.

Nancy dropped her phone and wiped at her face.

The new Dr. Harvey glanced pointedly down at his watch. "I guess I shouldn't be surprised."

Nancy blinked at him. She looked out the window at the street as if some explanation for his appearance would materialize there.

"Sorry." He rubbed at his forehead. "I was walking by and I saw you sitting in the window."

"Of course." She was dumbstruck. She shifted on the stool, which was not very comfortable under normal circumstances, which these were not.

"I thought I'd say hello," he said.

Nancy looked down at her bourbon. God, he was right. She was drinking and it was barely past eleven.

"Hello," he said.

He was wearing a navy-blue cardigan today. Did he have a whole closet full? She imagined stepping inside, running her hands across the rows of cashmere. This close, she could smell him. Sandalwood. And cedar. The new Dr. Harvey was delicious.

"Hello," she said.

"I won't keep you." He took a step backward.

"No." She gestured at the empty table. "Sit down. There's plenty of room."

"I couldn't."

"You could," she said. "It's practically illegal for me to sit at this table by myself." She pointed at the sign taped to the table, which specified it was for four or more only.

"You're not waiting for someone?" He glanced toward the door.

"My daughter, but she won't mind. The more the merrier."

He put his hand on one of the stools, that eyebrow raised again. "You're sure?"

She smiled. "A thing you should know about East-siders is that we're blunt. If we say it's okay, it's okay."

"Okay, then." He gave a quick nod and pulled out the stool, climbing into it with much more ease than Nancy had. She would have to remember to make sure he was gone before she dismounted.

Carole King's voice faded and Nancy didn't recognize the next song. She glanced at her phone. Where was Liz? She had no idea what to say to the new Dr. Harvey. Why had she asked him to sit? She didn't even know this man's first name. And there was a good chance she had mascara smeared down her face.

Across from her, the new Dr. Harvey stared out the window. One finger tapped against the table and Nancy concentrated on the rhythm. A song? Or just a random tic? It didn't matter. This was all a horrible mistake. She fought the urge to raise her bourbon glass to her lips and down it all in one gulp.

"I'm David, by the way." He glanced at her and then back out the window, like he was suddenly shy. Or regretting his decision to sit down. "David Harvey."

Nancy nodded. David. Had she known that? It didn't sound right to her. The old Dr. Harvey's first name had been Harold. Harold Harvey. He'd delivered Chris, her first boy, before he had retired. So long ago. She sighed.

"Well, I'm—," she started to say.

"Nancy." David leaned forward, that smirk back on his face. "I know who you are."

She tilted her head. "Do you?" *How? How did he know? Had he asked around about her?* She was notorious in town, if not famous.

"Of course," he said.

Nancy laughed. She imagined the feel of his cardigan slipping between her fingers.

Out the window, Liz rounded the corner. Her daughter waved her hand in that funny way she did, as if she was afraid to make a gesture too big. Where had she learned that? Not from Stan and surely not from her.

Nancy took another sip of her bourbon and let the silky liquid linger on her tongue.

There'd been no bourbon on that trip to the Baltic. Vodka only, though it was smoky in a way she'd never tasted since. For the longest time she'd tried to find something that recreated that flavor before giving up. But maybe she should try again. Go to one of the big liquor stores in Louisville. Try every bottle of vodka on the shelf. Why not?

She tilted her bourbon glass back and forth in front of the new Dr. Harvey. In front of David.

"Well, if you know who I am, then you'll know I need another bourbon." Then she winked at him, surprised her face still remembered the motion.

The Virginia Woolf Room

For Rachel, it was all about the Virginia Woolf Room. Once she knew it existed, she had to go. She had to be in that space.

"We could just go to London, you know," Charlie said. They were in their living room, Rachel on the couch and Charlie in his chair, warm under blankets and cats. "Actually see Virginia Woolf's house in Bloomsbury. Or Monk's House in the country." Charlie was an English professor. He'd spent a whole year in London when he was in graduate school.

"But you can't *stay* in her houses," Rachel said.

"No, you cannot," Charlie said.

"Exactly," Rachel said. She would go to Florida instead. An island in the gulf off the coast of Sarasota. The Gloria Beach Hotel, a whole building with every room themed around an author, and the Virginia Woolf Room would be hers.

"There's a writing thing." Rachel showed Charlie the webpage. "I'll apply to that."

"Or you could just go," he said. "Because you wanted to."

"No, that would be frivolous."

"Okay." Charlie laughed. "But you have to, you know, get in. Write something."

"No big deal." She blew up the tiny thumbnail image of the room on her phone and tried to make out the pattern on the bedspread.

Were those flowers? What kind? What kind of flowers would Virginia Woolf have on her bedspread?

"You're not a writer though," Charlie said.

"I read a lot of books." She shrugged. "How hard can it be?"

>>

Rachel bought a notebook at the Dollar General one afternoon when she stopped in for toilet paper. Before the pandemic, she'd let them get down to one roll. Never again. Their closet was always full of toilet paper now, just one of the small ways her world had shifted and would never go back.

She stuck the little notebook in the bag she took to work at the Main Street Saloon. In slow moments, she wrote down snippets of conversation. People still speculating about the sex survey from back in January. Gossip about Nancy and the new Dr. Harvey's scandalous relationship.

Joshua was a waiter and cranky. She made him the main character. But, in her story, he was even crankier, which often passed for deep. The story ended with a bar brawl, which she had never actually seen at the Saloon, but always secretly hoped for. It was fun to imagine the scene, to guess who would throw punches and who would hang back and watch.

She sent the story in and a month later, the organizer called to tell her she was the second person accepted to the writer's workshop. Thankfully, the first person chose the Dr. Seuss Room. Let them have it. The Virginia Woolf Room was all hers.

"Can I read your story?" Charlie asked.

"Maybe," Rachel said.

>>

The first time Rachel had read *To the Lighthouse*, she had hated every word. The plot? A batty woman wandered from one room to the other in her vacation house. Her son wondered whether they would take the boat out. Her husband? He was an asshole, but the woman clearly didn't see it. In the middle of the book, everything stopped and the house started talking? Not to mention the weirdness of Lily, the painter, obsessing over one stroke on her canvas. That was a big deal? *That* made a book?

Rachel had read *To The Lighthouse* in a philosophy and literature class, which had wiped out two requirements at once. That had been a plus. But the books the professor had required had been horrible. Rachel had never known books could be both so boring and so confusing. Gertrude Stein. Walker Percy. Virginia Woolf.

"Woolf's experimenting with stream of consciousness," the professor had explained. He'd been skinny with a long gray ponytail. "She practically invented stream of consciousness in the modern novel, trying to capture the very experience of thinking itself."

"That's not what it sounds like when I think," Rachel had said. She'd been fearless in her student days. In her forties now, she missed that fearlessness but also thought it had been exhausting for everyone else, including the philosophy professor.

"You don't think so?" the professor had asked. "Have you ever tried to write your thoughts down? Not an edited version. Not a cleaned-up, grammatically correct, full sentences and paragraphs sort of version. Just a garbage dump of thoughts on paper? How do you think that would sound?"

"Better than this," Rachel had mumbled.

She'd still hated the book, even after she finished it, but she hadn't sold it back to the bookstore at the end of the semester. She'd kept it, along with all the notes she'd made from class written in the margins, directions for how to make sense of the chaos. She'd marked the passages where the husband was apparently drawing on some famous philosopher. The places where Lily stood in as a representation for the oppression of all women artists.

After one of her many post-college moves, Rachel had pulled the book out and read it again. She was twenty-seven then and she had considered maybe that *was* what thoughts were like. Maybe there *was* something sad about never getting to the lighthouse. At a museum gift shop, she had bought a postcard with a photo of Woolf and her sister, the painter Vanessa Bell. She'd stuck it on the wall of an apartment, the one in Cincinnati. She read a Woolf biography. She'd woken up sometimes and the first thing she'd seen when she opened her eyes was Virginia and Vanessa. They came to feel like people she knew.

>>

Rachel flew into Tampa the night before the writer's conference began. The next day they would take a bus down to the island, an hour-and-a-half drive south along the coast. She hadn't traveled by herself since she and Charlie got married, ten years ago. She hadn't flown since the pandemic. Waiting in the airport and on the plane, she felt like someone else was taking this trip. She felt like that a lot now, like she was watching her own life from the outside.

On the shuttle from the airport, she thought about the Saloon and that tomorrow it would open without her. Liz and Nancy would come for lunch and she would not be there to pour Nancy her favorite bourbon. The thought was thrilling and terrifying in equal measures.

She went for dinner by herself that night instead of with the other workshop people. They had set up a group chat, which she quickly silenced while she sat on a patio beside the water and dipped grouper nuggets in a roasted red pepper aioli. Fish did not taste like this in Indiana. Back home, there were months left yet between her and the first day it would be warm enough to sit outside. Even then, the only water was the river, which always smelled a little stale.

She tried one of the fancy margaritas, thinking of Nancy. It came with a burnt orange peel that she hated at first but that grew on her. She read the literary magazine they'd sent her with her registration packet, published by the press that sponsored the workshop. The stories were okay. She didn't think they were much better or worse than her own. Was writing really that easy?

She had two cocktails and then texted Charlie good night because there was no sense calling him. He was bad on the phone. The next morning, she put on a tank top she'd packed and a light sweater in case it was too cold. She glanced at her hair in the mirror—curled and frizzed in the humidity, instead of the flat mess it was back home. And then—why not?—she put on sunscreen, breathing in the sweet coconut smell.

>>

There wasn't much to see on the ride to the island until the bus turned west and followed a road that ran along the coast. That was when Rachel spotted the birds, half-hidden in the weeds along a drainage ditch.

"Oh, look at those birds." She pointed out the window. The older woman beside her craned her neck to see, but the birds were already gone. "Those looked like storks."

"Storks?" the woman said.

"Maybe," Rachel said.

She had birding ambitions. She liked to look at guidebooks. Charlie had bought her a pair of binoculars for Christmas one year. There was a wildlife refuge in the next town over that was a big migration stop. She told herself every spring and fall that she would get up early and drive over with her binoculars one weekend. Those were the kinds of things she wanted to spend her time on now that the pandemic was over, not scrolling endlessly through her phone. She hadn't made the trip yet, but she knew what a stork looked like.

"Could that have been a stork?" Rachel leaned toward the bus driver, who was presumably a local. "Are there storks down here?"

The driver shrugged. "It's all just big birds to me."

She leaned back into her seat. "I think it was a stork." What kind though? Were they migratory, stopping in Florida on their way to somewhere more exotic?

"Which workshop are you in?" the older woman beside her asked.

"The fiction one," Rachel said. The bird had been mostly white, but had its head been dark? It had passed so quickly. She didn't have a guidebook, but she could download one of those birding apps on her phone.

"Novel or short story?" the woman asked.

"Short story," Rachel said.

"Oh, that means you're with Beth Clark." The woman sighed. "So jealous. She's so amazing. I can't believe they got her to come. She never does these sorts of things."

Rachel nodded. "Yeah. I know."

Rachel did not know. She'd read none of Beth Clark's stories before she sent in her piece. She had recognized the name of one of Beth Clark's books. It had been made into a Netflix series. She hadn't watched that either. Beth Clark's bio included a long list of impressive awards, but Rachel wasn't into short stories. She'd written one, yes, but only so she could stay in the Virginia Woolf Room.

"You're going to have such an amazing week," the woman said.

"I know," Rachel said. She was. Because she'd be in the Virginia Woolf Room.

>>

Rachel woke in the night, her mouth dry. She'd had too many beers at the reception. She hadn't drunk enough water. It was hard to stay hydrated. Now, as she hauled herself out of bed and stumbled to the tiny bathroom to pee, she thought she could feel the beginnings of a urinary tract infection.

"Fuck," she muttered. She hadn't brought any of the cranberry pills Charlie had researched and special-ordered for her. She was supposed to take them every day to prevent UTIS, but she didn't. She was headed toward that age where she had to purchase a pill organizer to keep track. She didn't want to be there yet.

She poured water into the tiny hotel glass and drank it down. Then did the same thing four more times. Maybe she could flush out the infection before it got any worse.

She looked at the time on her phone. A little before six. When she pulled the curtains back on the window that faced the water, she could see the beginnings of the dark blue that came just before dawn. The sun would rise earlier down here, even in the depths of February.

When they'd finally gotten to the island yesterday, they'd all been shuffled off to a reception to do yet more getting acquainted. By the time the reception ended, it was dark and she had been too overwhelmed to fully take in the details of the Virginia Woolf Room.

Now, in the dim light of the lamp that sat on a bedside table, she saw that it was small, barely enough space for the double bed, a dresser, and a tiny desk. The color scheme was brighter than she'd imagined—muted yellows and oranges with a geometric pattern stenciled around the ceiling. She wondered if the pattern was copied from something Vanessa Bell had painted. Small photos of Virginia looking plaintive or sad hung on the wall. The top of the desk was lined with Woolf's novels and essays.

There was nothing pink at all. Why had she thought it should be pink? Was it the softness in the photos of Virginia Woolf's face? The image of the flowers Mrs. Dalloway was forever carrying around or arranging? Why did she think of Virginia Woolf as pink?

She dressed and went outside to walk the beach. She pulled one of the guest chairs out and sat. She Googled "white stork with dark head." "A wood stork," she whispered. They liked wetlands, so she probably wouldn't see one on the beach. But there was a preserve on the island she'd seen on a map. The hotel had bikes. Maybe she could ride one over there and look for storks.

>>

There was something about the quality of light in the Virginia Woolf Room. Or maybe it was the humidity. Or the displacement of being so far outside her own life. Rachel wasn't sure. She just knew that, day by day, she teetered on the edge of a deep hole inside her that she'd never realized was there. Some part of her wanted nothing more than to fall into it. What had saved her from it all these years? The trappings of a life. Another shift at the Saloon. Getting up to get Sam off to school before she'd moved to Bloomington for college. Another visit Rachel had to make to her parents even though it was all obligation. There was nothing but obligation. Obligation was all that held her together. Now, sitting in the compressed space of the Virginia Woolf Room, she could let go. She wanted to let go of it all and see what happened next.

The workshops were torture, but she couldn't bring herself to stop going. What would Charlie say? She'd paid all this money just to sit on the beach and stare out at the water? To hide in her room reading the books and novels off the shelf, devouring them one by one without being able to say what they were about as soon as she closed the cover? She woke up in the middle of the night to write feverishly in the little notebook that all the participants had gotten, her handwriting illegible in the morning, words and sentences that Rachel couldn't recognize as her own. Gibberish, as if a demon were whispering in her ear. Maybe that was all writing was.

The only thing she looked forward to about the workshops were the snacks. An endless supply of individual bags of chips and apples and oranges and protein bars. A carafe full of hot water and a large assortment of teas. The ritual of filling her bag with snacks and making her paper cup of tea at the beginning of each workshop was all that kept Rachel going. It was the small thing that stood between her and the void.

She became particularly fond of one type of granola bar—almond with a creamy yogurt coating. She sat in their assigned room one morning before workshop, chewing slowly, her hands cupped around her tea, staring out the window at the brightness of the Florida sun and the patterns of shadow cast by the palm leaves. She held tight to the slow motion of her jaw, the sound of crunching inside her skull, the way her tongue could distinguish the almonds from the oats. If she focused on her tea and the gra-nola bar, she could build a protective bubble between her and the other people in the workshop, their small talk an annoying buzzing in her ear.

"What do you think?" a voice beside her said.

Rachel swallowed the last bit of granola bar but still felt empty. She hoped there would be more after the workshop was over. It was day five and they were all waiting for Beth Clark to arrive at the workshop room. Beth Clark was always late.

"I'm sorry?" Rachel said. The words scraped coming out of her mouth. She couldn't remember the last time she'd spoken. She imagined her lips and mouth crusted over with saltwater.

"What do you think of Beth Clark as a workshop leader?" It was the older woman who looked like Pam from the Saloon. Rachel had forgotten all their names immediately. Deliberately.

She ran her fingers across her mouth, feeling for crumbs. "She's great," she said. She crumpled the granola-bar wrapper and shoved it in her bag.

"Do you really think so though?" asked a younger woman who reminded her a little of Sam's friend Emily.

Rachel scanned the faces of the people in the room. It was hard to focus. What did they want from her? She glanced out the window again, wondering if she could just slip out the door.

"No?" Rachel whispered.

What was happening? They'd all been so excited the first four days. They were giddy every time Beth Clark walked into the room, late or not. At lunch, which Beth Clark did not eat with them, they repeated everything Beth Clark had said, digesting it, turning each sentence this way and that. They studied each utterance with the intensity Rachel's mom brought to the clothes racks at the Goodwill, examining every shirt for a hole or a frayed cuff. Searching every bin for that designer blouse with the tags still on, never worn. *They were all so lucky to be in the workshop with Beth Clark*, they'd repeated over and over again like a mantra.

They needed something from Beth Clark or from each other or the place. They needed so much. Everyone always needed so much, all while pretending so hard that they didn't. Rachel watched it every day in the Saloon. It was so familiar and so exhausting. Rachel wanted them to leave her alone, but they were staring at her. Waiting.

"She tells everyone the same thing," the lone man in the group said. "*Your writing is amazing. Keep going.*"

"It doesn't mean anything if she says it to everyone," not-Emily said.

Rachel laughed, then covered her mouth to hold it in. "Right," she said.

"You don't think so?" the man said. "What did she say to you about your story?"

"Oh, not much." Rachel shrugged.

Beth Clark had met with them one on one after their piece was workshopped, two stories per day. Everyone got ten minutes, except on the day they'd talked about Rachel's story, when the discussion of the other story for that day had gone long, leaving Rachel only seven minutes after they were done. She had sat in the chair next to Beth Clark for only five. She could barely remember what Beth Clark had said. She remembered the sound of rustling as Beth Clark flipped through the pages of Rachel's story. She pointed to one sentence or the other. Rachel tried to pay attention, because Charlie might ask her what she'd said, but Rachel was distracted by imagining the feel of sand under her feet. The sooner she was done with Beth Clark, the sooner she could get back to the beach. To the room. To that hole inside herself that had its own gravitational force, calling, calling. Always calling.

"Someone from the memoir workshop asked Beth if she could use her as a reference for a writer's residency," the man said.

"What did she say?" not-Emily asked.

"To get in touch with her publicist," the man said.

"This isn't what I paid for," not-Pam said.

Rachel laughed again. This time she didn't stop herself. She let it out.

"Why is that funny?" the man asked. He looked at not-Pam. "What's funny? What's so funny?"

Rachel covered her mouth to stop the laughter and stared at the story they were supposed to workshop that day, sitting on the table in front of her. Words and words and words, written across the paper.

"I write because it's the closest I can come to getting inside other people's heads," Beth Clark had said earlier that week. Rachel could understand that, but, also, being inside people's heads was so exhausting. Guessing whether Liz wanted another drink or if Sam was upset about something and keeping it to herself, letting it fester inside. Rachel didn't want to be inside these people's heads. Their need tugged at her. Their need filled the room until it was stifling.

"What do you want?" Rachel whispered. She didn't care if they could hear her or not. She didn't want to talk to them. She didn't want to talk to anyone. "Do you even know?"

"What'd she say?" the man asked. He was yelling now.

Rachel could feel them turning on her. She shoved the pages of the story into her bag and stood, just as Beth Clark at last drifted in.

"No," Rachel said. She brushed past Beth Clark and out the door.

"Where is she going?" she heard Beth Clark say as the door shut behind her, but Rachel felt the Florida sun on her face and did not care.

>>

Rachel thought about renting a bike and going in search of the wood stork, but she didn't. She didn't want to be that far away from the small space of the room and the beach. The birds she saw she called by their simplest names. Gull. Sandpiper. Smaller sandpiper. Crane. Crane with yellow feet. Pelican. The details didn't matter.

She sat in one of the beach chairs, staring at the words she'd written in her notebook the night before. She'd woken with the sure sense that a great revelation had come to her and must be recorded. An idea that changed everything. But what she had written was a description of the way Joshua the waiter danced sometimes when a certain song came on at the Saloon. The way he closed his eyes and swayed his hips and moved his hands in a tiny swirling motion. He was a ridiculous man and when he danced like that, Rachel laughed and laughed. All of them did.

"I'm bringin' it," Joshua would say, his eyes closed, his lips pursed. "See me bring it?"

How was that a revelation?

Rachel had skipped workshop and so far there were no consequences that she could see. She hadn't talked to Charlie in days—she couldn't remember how many—and there had been a certain desperation in his last voice message, which she had chosen to ignore.

She almost nodded off in the chair—she wasn't sleeping well, what with the writing in the middle of the night—so when she opened her eyes and saw the duck, she thought at first she was dreaming. She sat up and shielded her eyes from the glare of the sun. No, it was still there. A duck. Not one of the white, domestic variety. A wild duck, with the green and brown pattern she'd seen on decoys and the paintings that seemed to be everywhere. Why did people like duck paintings so much?

She looked up and down the beach, but she was alone. There was no one to share her duck sighting. No one to ask whether this was normal or not. It was the first duck she'd seen on the beach. Didn't they prefer ponds or lakes? And why was the duck by itself? Didn't they travel in groups? Or flocks? What was a group of ducks called?

Rachel stood and walked toward the water. It was a still day, but there were gentle waves. The duck lifted and fell on the swells. It floated, but didn't seem to be moving down the beach. She imagined its legs under the water, paddling like mad against the tide and the current just to keep itself in the same spot. It was unnatural, she realized, to see one duck like this. She wanted to find the other ducks, the ones who had abandoned this one, and punish them. But there were no other ducks in sight.

"What are you doing?" she called to the duck. "Why are you all alone?"

She studied the sky inland and out in the gulf. Pelicans swooped down low over the waves and then rose again in groups of twos or threes. A flock of what she'd decided to call the smaller gulls hovered over the water before diving and falling, then rising with the silver flash of fish in their mouths. None of them showed the least bit of interest in the duck. There was no squadron of ducks on the horizon, coming to rescue their comrade. It was just this one.

Rachel pulled out her phone. The duck needed help, clearly. Its solitude was dangerous. Who did you call about a lone duck on the beach? She stared at her phone for what felt like an hour but was only minutes. She waited for something to happen. For the duck to leave. For someone else to come along and tell her it was nothing to worry about.

In the end, she called Charlie.

"Hey, how's the beach?" he asked.

She could barely hear his voice over the sound of the waves. The duck didn't move. Or it did. It was working so hard. Was it sick? Injured? Rejected?

"It's all alone." Rachel could barely get the words out. Something was stealing her breath. Sobs. "Charlie, it's all alone. What do I do?"

"Rachel, what happened?" Charlie asked. She could hear the panic in his voice. "Are you okay?"

"No," she moaned. "No, I'm not."

>>

"Why did you go to a writer's conference?" Nancy asked.

Rachel was back in the bar, pouring Nancy's bourbon. It was Taco Tuesday. The place was packed. She didn't have time to explain to Nancy about the Virginia Woolf Room.

"It was in Florida," Rachel said instead. "It was warm. On the beach."

Nancy raised her bourbon glass. "Here's to the beach."

"To the beach." Rachel clinked the bottle against Nancy's glass and resisted the urge to take a drink. She lost herself in the familiar tasks of mixing margaritas and taking taco orders. All the regulars were there and a lot of them asked her where she'd been last week or how Florida was or why she'd come back to this February cold and gloom. She nodded or laughed or gave one-word answers. She didn't tell any of them about how after she'd called Charlie in incoherent tears, she'd booked an early flight and come home. She didn't tell them she woke up every morning still thinking about the duck. She didn't tell them what she'd learned in those days, that she was broken inside. That something had broken her.

"It's good to be home, though, isn't it?" Liz asked.

The crowd had thinned at last. Rachel was winded. She'd forgotten how exhausting the rush was.

"You missed us, right?" Liz was looking at her phone, only half-listening for Rachel's answer.

"Sure." Rachel stared at her fingers, which more and more did not look like they belonged to her.

She hadn't though. She hadn't missed them. That wasn't why she'd found herself sobbing on the beach. She hadn't missed Liz or Nancy or her shifts at the Saloon. She hadn't really missed Charlie that much.

Yes, she had felt strange and like she'd suddenly found a labyrinth inside herself, but coming home hadn't changed that. She hadn't wanted to leave the Virginia Woolf Room. She wanted to stay there, beside the beach, wandering that labyrinth forever.

There was no beach in Lanier, but sometimes she wandered down to the river, letting the quiet of the streets fall around her like a blanket. She took her notebook with her and wrote. She wrote more descriptions of Joshua. Of what the bar felt like when a really good band was playing. The drowsiness of a slow afternoon. She filled the pages until she felt sleepy and then she went back home and crawled into bed with Charlie, her mind empty enough to sleep, as if the sentences themselves had been taking up room.

>>

Rachel looked up from slicing limes for garnish to find the Saloon was empty, the afternoon sunlight bright through the front windows. She put down her knife and walked to one of the big tables that sat in the window. She picked up a beer bottle Joshua had forgotten to bus. She stopped and stood, the sun on her face. It wasn't Florida, but it was an early spring light, the kind that was especially clear, like the way the world looked after she finally got new glasses. That sense of all the details she'd been missing filled in at last.

Outside, an older man made his way down the sidewalk, walking bow-legged, like a cowboy. He stopped and hauled himself up into a truck parked in front of the Saloon. Through the window, Rachel saw a dog stand up in the front seat. It must have been lying there the entire time, waiting for the man's return. The dog's whole body swayed in a rocking motion as its tail wagged—a slow wag for an old dog. Rachel could see the gray in its muzzle.

The old man put his keys in the ignition, then with one hand draped on the steering wheel, cupped the dog's head with the other. It was a reflex gesture. Automatic. Not so much a pat as an absent-minded caress.

The truck started. The dog lay down. The old man pulled out onto Main Street and disappeared.

"I have to write this down," Rachel thought. She didn't have her notebook with her. She pulled out one of the cocktail napkins. She was such a cliché. She wrote, "The old man and his dog." She folded the napkin and put it in her pocket. She went about refilling the ketchup bottles and wiping down the tables. She was easing the way for the night shift, which was her job but also a way to restore order to the chaos, over and over again.

When she got home, Charlie was still on campus. The house was empty. She picked up the young adult novel she was reading, then set it down. She pulled the napkin out of her pocket.

Her notebook was in Sam's room, where she'd left it one night when she couldn't sleep. She'd sat at Sam's old rolltop desk and reread the notes on Joshua she'd written on the beach. Her obser-vations during workshop. She'd written down a funny story Liz had told her at the bar that day. Half the notebook was full and that felt satisfying. It felt like progress, even if she wasn't sure toward what.

She crawled into Sam's bed, a cup of tea beside her. She liked the view out Sam's windows, different from her and Charlie's bedroom. She could almost pretend she was somewhere else. She ran her hand over the napkin, smoothing it out against the blanket.

What would Charlie think if he came home and found her here? Did she care?

She hovered the pen over the page. Wrote a word. Crossed it out.

That day on the beach, she'd managed to calm down enough to explain to Charlie about the duck. She'd told him how she'd stopped going to the workshops.

"Do you want to come home?" he'd asked. "Do you need to come home?"

She hadn't been sure what the answer was. She still wasn't. She had come home because she'd known otherwise Charlie would worry about her. His worry would become hers. It was easiest to take a plane home.

But that day, with the duck, she hadn't yet decided. And when she'd looked up from her conversation with Charlie, the duck was gone. Had it sunk into the ocean? Flown away? Had she imagined it all along?

She blew across the surface of her tea and stared at the napkin. It was too hard to take what she'd seen that afternoon and convert it into words. They would never be right. She would never be able to translate the sweetness or the intimacy of the man and his dog. Everything about the old man's life distilled down into that moment. Or maybe nothing at all about his life. Maybe she knew nothing about him. But her heart said no. Her heart told her that moment was everything. What could words do with that? Nothing. They failed. The words would always fail.

She sat her pen down and took another sip of tea, though it had already grown cold.

"Just find one true moment," Beth Clark had told them in workshop one day. "Always start there."

Rachel closed her eyes and tried to remember the old man's face. The exact motion of his hand as it moved across the dog's head.

That day at the beach, she'd waded out into the water. She hadn't known why. Perhaps she'd thought she could find the duck somehow. Save it.

The water had been so much colder than she thought it would be. She'd held up the skirt she was wearing, but its edges got wet. She went in up to her knees and then her thighs and then her waist. She had waited for someone along the shore to call her back, but no one had.

The waves kept coming. It all just kept coming. The pandemic ended and they all just went on. She went away. She came home. It never stopped.

She'd stood for a long time in the water. The bottoms of her feet had been wrinkled when she came out. She could barely feel her toes. She still wasn't sure what had made her turn again for the shore.

She picked up the pen. Wrote a word. Another. Strokes and strokes on the page.

Time stopped. When Charlie came home, she didn't hear him call her name. She was already gone.

Joyce, Alone

The truth was, Joyce liked it when Don was gone.

This was the realization she'd come to two years into the pandemic and two weeks into Don's disappearance out of her life and into the Covid ward as she'd sat in Don's chair in their living room. She'd never realized what a beautiful view he had out the front window. From Don's chair, she'd been able to see all the way across the valley to the Kentucky shore, and in the early spring when the trees were still bare, a peek of the river down below. They'd lived in the house for thirty-three years and she had no idea that view was out there. From her usual chair, all you could see was the wall where the TV hung and Don.

Joyce liked sitting in Don's chair. She would take a small stack of pecan sandies on a plate resting on her stomach, all for her, which she would dunk in a glass of milk. That was breakfast. No need to make anything more elaborate when it was just her. For dinner, she'd have a simple turkey sandwich and potato chips, at seven thirty, which had been way too late for Don's relentless appetite.

She would call the kids and the grandkids and talk to them without Don's large presence looming behind her. They would whisper secrets in their soft voices that she would be able to hear without the sound of the TV Don kept on all the time. She liked having the children all to herself.

Joyce had been enjoying Don's absence and this meant she was a horrible person, because Don had been in the hospital, fighting for his life against the Covid and she'd sat in his chair as she'd watched the barges pass on the river through the window, a small, contented smile on her face.

She was surely going to hell.

>>

Those Don-less days weren't enough time for Joyce to build a whole new life, and, anyway, year two of the pandemic wasn't any safer, according to her daughter, Heather, so Joyce couldn't see as much of the kids and the grandkids as she would have liked. They were being so careful.

"We don't want to expose Dad," Heather kept saying. "Or you, Mom."

"Don't worry about me," Joyce said. She didn't worry. Joyce wasn't worried about herself at all. She knew in her bones that if she got Covid, it would be nothing. She wouldn't end up in the hospital like Don. She came from peasant stock, compact and hearty, not like the fragile waifs in Don's family.

Plus, women were just tougher than men, and Covid was no different. She'd read it in an article, that men got much sicker and were more likely to die than women. They were thinking about treating men with estrogen at one point and that made her laugh out loud.

"What's so funny?" Don had asked. This was a year before he'd gotten sick. This was in April, just a month into the whole thing, when they thought the virus would never reach Lanier. When they watched the morning news while they sat at the kitchen table and shook their heads or laughed at the world gone crazy.

"Men," she said. "Men are funny."

"What?"

"Nothing."

Two and a half weeks wasn't enough to build a whole other life, but it was enough to feel the places where life with Don pinched at her, like the way her stomach felt when she took her panty hose off after the boring and endless hour at West Lanier Church on Sunday. The panty hose didn't hurt exactly. She could still breathe with the panty hose on. Heather had convinced her to stop wearing the control top at least.

But Joyce couldn't pretend it didn't feel fantastic to walk in the house and pull off the panty hose first thing, before her dress. Sometimes before she even made it to the bedroom. She couldn't ignore the red creases the panty hose left across the soft, white flesh of her stomach. Her stomach that had been different so many years ago. Not better. Joyce didn't want that young stomach back. She didn't want to be twenty again. But it certainly seemed panty hose hadn't bothered her as much back then.

That was Don. He was like panty hose. Constricting. A little less comfortable as the years went on.

So, yes, the house was empty without him. But also bigger. More spacious. And with a better view.

>>

It was while Don was in the hospital that Heather signed Joyce up for the online painting and drawing class. It wasn't a secret. Obviously, Heather knew. But it wasn't something Joyce told Don about either.

"I can't do that with your father fighting for his life," Joyce said when Heather first suggested the class. Don had been in the hospital three weeks by then.

"Fighting for his life." That was what everyone said. Don was "fighting for his life." Sometimes, Joyce pictured him in a boxing match with death, which did not improve Don's odds of winning.

Nothing that she saw on their video calls suggested Don was fighting anything. They weren't allowed to visit him in the Covid ward. On the screen of Heather's tablet, which showed Don's room, Don barely moved. He was hardly ever awake. He was a small creature, barely existing in the center of a loud forest of machinery.

"But what are you doing to help him?" she'd asked the doctor after Don had been in there for ten days. "What are you actually *doing*?"

"There's not a lot we can do, Mrs. Blankman," Dr. Barrett said.

She had no idea how old Dr. Barrett was. Twenty? Sixty? White? Asian? There was no way to tell. She'd seen Dr. Barrett only once, back in late May, when Don passed out and she'd ignored his protests that he was just fine during the entire drive to the hospital, where Don disappeared inside. Dr. Barrett's whole face had been covered by a mask and a surgical cap and eyeglasses that were tinted so she couldn't even tell what color his eyes were. His hands were gloved. Dr. Barrett could have been a robot for all Joyce could tell. His voice was about as expressive.

"We don't have a lot to throw at Covid right now," Dr. Barrett said when she managed to get him on the phone.

"So we just wait?" She wanted to drive up to the hospital and rip off all of Dr. Barrett's protective gear. Go to his house and stand in his driveway screaming until he made Don better.

"We just wait," Dr. Barrett said. "And give Don all the help we can to fight this off, right?"

"Right," Joyce said.

Don the fighter. He would love that, but Joyce wasn't so sure.

>>

"There's nothing else for you to do, Mom," Heather told her. "You might as well keep yourself busy. Keep yourself sane."

"But a painting class?" Joyce asked.

"You like to do those coloring books on your phone."

What did that have to do with painting? Joyce didn't have an artistic bone in her body. She wasn't going to do the class. She had zero intention of doing the class. It was a nice thought in the interfering way of bossy first-born children like Heather. And Joyce was a good, Midwestern woman, so she didn't out and out say no. She changed the subject or said she'd think about it. She didn't bring it up at all until Heather texted that she was out on their porch and Joyce opened the door to find her masked and holding a large shopping bag.

"Canvas. Paints. Brushes." Heather held the bag up. Joyce thought she might be smiling. It was hard to tell with the mask. "You're all set."

"Oh, Heather, you shouldn't have done that." Joyce stepped out onto the porch and Heather set the bag down and took a step back. "For heaven's sake, come in and have a cup of coffee, will you?"

"No, Mom. We talked about this."

Joyce started to argue but gave up. All conversations at a distance were ridiculous and an argument was even more so.

"I texted you the time and the link," Heather said. "You're all signed up. Thursdays at seven."

"That's too much, Heather. How much did it cost?"

"It's free. Through the library."

Joyce tried to think of another argument but nothing came. She eased into the wicker chair that sat on the front porch, decaying and unused. It creaked ominously.

"Can't you just sit here for a moment with me?" Joyce nodded toward the porch swing. "Outside is safe, right?"

Heather stared at Joyce and then at the porch swing. She let out a great, exasperated sigh before she climbed onto the porch and sat. The swing groaned but held.

"I know it's hard, Mom," Heather said. "I just thought this would help."

They tried to talk to Don every night on the phone. They had to get a nurse to set it up and sometimes the nurses were too busy. Joyce couldn't be mad at them. And Heather called her every day. She brought the kids over when she could. It was more than some of her friends' children were doing, and Joyce knew she should be grateful. But she wanted to *see* them. Their whole faces. Could she convince Heather to take off the mask?

"I guess I'll give the class a try, since you spent all this money." Joyce picked at a place where the wicker weave of the chair had come undone.

She watched a vine that was climbing up the box hedge wave in the breeze. She needed to weed the front bed. She'd regret it if she didn't. The vines would take over. It was a constant battle and the vines would always win. They were the real fighters.

She'd let the whole front of the house go and what must the neighbors think? These wicker chairs were old and rotting where the rain blew in on them. They needed to be replaced. She didn't usually make any major purchases without consulting Don first, but that didn't matter now, did it? She hated these chairs, inherited from Don's aunt's front porch when she died. They were useless. Uncomfortable. What was the point of buying chairs no one ever meant to sit in?

>>

When Heather left (mask still firmly in place), Joyce hauled the bag of paints and brushes inside and left it in the foyer. She sent Don a text she had no idea if he would see. She tried to read in bed, but it was quiet without Don and the TV and whatever game he'd be watching.

She turned off the lights and lay in the dark. She tried to picture Don in the hospital, but she was tired of the effort it took to imagine a connection between them. Every day their lives drifted further and further apart. Was he even thinking of her? Or did he have Julie Davis to comfort him on the Covid ward?

Yes, Joyce knew about Julie Davis. Along with everyone else in the town. She'd waited for Don to make a big pronouncement all those years ago—that he was leaving her. Or he wanted a divorce. It would be hard, but, also, there would be freedom. She could get rid of the TV in their bedroom, which she hadn't wanted in the first place. Store the glasses in the cupboard upside down, like they were supposed to be, instead of right side up, which was how Don's mother had done it. She'd never have to listen to Don running water the whole time he brushed his teeth or on the rare occasion he decided to wash a dish. So wasteful, all that water.

"Joyce doesn't like for me to wash the dishes," she'd heard him tell a friend, smiling like a jackal. "She's old-fashioned that way."

No, you ass, she wanted to say. *I just hate the way you do the dishes.*

Julie Davis would find it delightful, no doubt.

"Fuck Don," she whispered. Then she laughed at the way the word sounded coming out of her mouth, like a language she might have been meant to speak all along.

She turned on the light, put on her slippers, and padded down to the foyer. She brought the bag of art supplies over to Don's chair and flipped on his lamp. She liked the way the living room felt, with just a small circle of light and her at the center.

She unpacked the bag slowly, absorbing the colors of the paint set. She inhaled the fresh-cut wood smell of the palette. She ran the soft bristles of the brushes against her cheeks and listened to the sound of the thick pages as she flipped through the sketchbook.

It all took up space, painting did. A place to put the paints. To set up the canvas until it dried. You had to commit part of your life to it and there had never been room before.

It took up space and now she had it to spare.

>>

Joyce set up on the sun porch for the first night of painting class. Of course, the sun had long since set, but Joyce told herself the memory of the bright light still lingered and that was good for her artistic debut.

Joyce was certain she'd never be able to figure out the link and the camera, and then she'd have an excuse to skip it altogether. But Heather had written detailed instructions and everything worked and, suddenly, Joyce was staring at the tiny faces of eleven other people and their instructor, Ross.

"Welcome to the class, Joyce!" Ross's tinny voice came through her computer.

"Oh." Joyce touched her hair. It looked so much different on the computer screen. Her skin was green. It was horrible. "Hello? Can you hear me?"

"We can," Ross said. "Let's have everyone introduce themselves before we get started."

Joyce wanted to lean close and squint at the little faces on the screen to see if there was anyone she knew, but if she did that, she'd have to look at her own enlarged face. Instead, she listened to everyone's introductions and there was only one name she recognized—Emily Butler, who she remembered as one of her students at the junior high. Everyone else was a stranger, which was a relief, if also puzzling. Were there really that many people in Lanier she didn't know?

"I have no idea what I'm doing," she wanted to say to Ross, the instructor, but there was no way she could figure out how to do it quietly. Privately. She had to just go along. So that's what she did as they worked on a still life—a green glass vase with a single rose. At the end, everyone could show their work if they wanted to, but no one had to. For that, Joyce was grateful. She didn't think her vase looked much like a vase and her rose was more daisy-ish, but the people in the class chatted as they worked and even if she didn't say much that first class, the murmuring sound of their voices in the sun porch was soothing. For the two hours the class lasted, she forgot about Don and the Covid and the pandemic. Her life reduced to the small square of canvas and color and that was enough.

>>

"Yard parties are okay." Joyce snipped off more of the unruly vine and shoved it into the compost bag. "I saw on the news. They said they're okay."

"I guess, Mom, but they say something different every week." Heather pulled a single weed out of the bed. At that rate, the weeding would take forever.

"So there's no reason to listen to anything they say because it'll just change tomorrow, right?" Joyce waved her hand in a flippant gesture. She felt flippant. She liked the word itself. Flippant. Flip-ping. Flip.

"I wouldn't go that far," Heather said.

Joyce shrugged. She was having some of the people from the painting class over tomorrow night. She didn't need Heather's approval for that. She was a sixty-five-year-old woman. She didn't need anyone's approval.

"Have you talked to Dr. Barrett lately?" Heather sat back on the sidewalk, as if pulling three weeds had just plumb worn her out. She'd at least let her mask fall down to her chin, even if she still wouldn't take it off.

Joyce blew out a quick puff of air. "No. You know how hard it is to get a hold of that man."

"Well, a nurse, at least?" Heather asked. "I mean, has there been any change?"

Joyce threw her clippers down with more force than she meant to. They stuck in the ground in a satisfying way.

What change? she wanted to say. He's either dead or better. What else was there to know?

"Do you want me to call?" Heather's voice was softer, like when she was little, asking if their house would be hit by a tornado, Joyce soothing her with the lie that tornadoes couldn't come to their neighborhood on the side of the hill because they weren't invited.

"Would you?" Joyce asked. "It would be such a help."

She had so much to do to get ready for the painting people.

>>

Joyce stood on her back porch and surveyed the yard as she waited for the first guests to arrive. She could admit that she may have gone overboard. Was it because she felt the need to compensate for the fact that they were in the backyard instead of inside the house? Maybe. It didn't stop her from deep-cleaning inside too. People would still need to go in for the bathroom, after all.

She paid for a one-off landscaping visit from Grass-Rite, the lawn service company their neighbors Kate and Jim used, the one Don cursed every time they showed up next door with a small army of short, dark-skinned men with leaf blowers and weed whackers.

"What kind of man doesn't mow his own lawn?" Don would grumble.

When Grass-Rite came, Joyce sat in her housedress on the back porch with her cup of coffee and watched the men go to work. "*Buenos dias*," she said to the one who edged the sidewalk. He glanced around, like he wasn't sure she was talking to him, then nodded.

Now the grass was, in fact, just right. Her lilies were starting to bloom and the ferns she'd bought at the nursery on the Hilltop were a perfect round, lush green. She'd gone a little crazy in the garden store the week before, buying fairy lights that were solar powered, so she didn't have to bother with wiring or plugs, which was Don's domain. She bought cushions for all the chairs, bright patterns in yellow and orange and blue that didn't even match, because shabby chic was a thing. She bought new chairs for the front porch—sturdy metal instead of wicker—but she'd pulled them around back for tonight. She'd need the extra seating. She bought lights that were shaped like butterflies to line the sidewalk and a little fountain that filled up a bucket and then dumped it out, over and over.

"Fountains just attract mosquitoes," she heard Don say inside her head.

Well, she'd also bought some sort of electronic devices that were supposed to use advanced technology to repel mosquitoes without killing them—the mechanics were fuzzy—but, *so there, Don!*

Now the first guests were trickling in and Joyce was greeting them in the pantsuit she'd bought at the new women's store in town, picked out for her especially by Rick, who was in the painting class and whose husband owned the store.

A pantsuit! She was wearing a pantsuit! All black, with the diamond earrings Don had bought her for their thirtieth anniversary!

"You look stunning." Rick kissed both her cheeks, which Heather would have found horrifying, but Heather wasn't here. Heather wasn't invited. "That suit was made for you."

Joyce beamed. "Cocktails right this way." She gestured toward the makeshift bar she'd set up, which Carol was manning, as promised, because Joyce knew nothing about cocktails. Don had always called Carol a boozehound, but look at how handy that was now.

Sometime after her second dirty martini (she hated the taste of the first one, but now it was fine, and she couldn't tell if that was because she'd gotten used to it or she was just drunk), Joyce wondered if her guests were making too much noise. Would Kate and Jim complain? Would they call the cops? Would they tell Heather? Would they tell Don, if they somehow managed to communicate with him up at his hospital bunker?

"Turn the music up!" Carol yelled from behind the bar. They'd run out of ice once already and sent Kyle, one of Nancy's grandsons, down to the liquor store for more. Kyle wasn't in the painting class, but he was there with Emily, the most talented artist in the group.

"Have you ever thought about getting a tattoo, Mrs. Blankman?"

Emily sat on one of the lounge chairs, like a queen on her divan, in a dress so short Joyce had to resist covering her with one of the blankets she'd put out, in case anyone got cold.

"Please call me Joyce, dear."

Emily had been a frequent visitor to her office when Joyce was the junior high guidance counselor. Emily had said she was there to get help with her course schedule, but then she'd lingered in a way that made Joyce wonder what secrets might be behind those bright, blue eyes.

"There's this great place in New Albany." Emily held out her arm, where the tattoo of a wispy centipede stretched from her wrist to her elbow. "They're such amazing artists, aren't they?"

Joyce touched one of the thin antennae on Emily's skin. As the guidance counselor, she was never allowed to touch the students. Not even to hug them when they broke down in sobs. But now she was just Joyce and they were both students. She could do as she pleased.

"I could never decide what to get." Joyce took another sip of her martini. "It would have to mean something, wouldn't it?"

What meant so much that she was willing to carry it around on her skin with her for the rest of her years on this earth? Not Don's name. Not the children or the grandchildren either. Joyce's life was more than one of those stickers people put in the back window of their mini-vans, announcing their whole family structure in stick figures for everyone to see.

"Oh, no, not at all." Emily had no drink. She told Joyce she'd had a gummy before she came, so she was fine, and Joyce was pretty sure she knew what that meant. "A tattoo doesn't have to mean anything. It's just art, you know. Something beautiful that you take with you everywhere. Always."

Joyce nodded. Yes, maybe she'd get a tattoo. Maybe she should finally retire from the high school and have more time to paint, like Ross, the teacher, suggested. Maybe she should buy a camper and become a nomad, which was what Emily and Kyle were going to do as soon as they saved up enough money.

The playlist Joyce had put together—subdued and tasteful—stopped mid-song. She took a step toward the Bluetooth speaker she'd set up. She could see Larry, Nancy's friend, bent over her computer. He straightened and the air filled with a song Joyce did not recognize, a song with a bass beat so strong her windows shook with the vibration.

"Dance party!" Larry yelled. He pulled Nancy into an empty space in the lawn and the two of them began to bounce, Larry more exuberantly than Nancy.

Joyce shrugged. So it was a dance party now. Who was she to fight it?

>>

Joyce didn't remember setting an alarm. Perhaps she'd done it before the party started. She certainly couldn't imagine she'd had the wherewithal to do it when she went to bed at last the night before, after everyone had left. There had been a moment, she could just remember, when it had seemed as if one of Emily's young friends might sleep on Joyce's couch and Joyce had to pretend this would be perfectly okay. No big deal. But then Nancy stepped in to give the child a ride and Joyce had resolved never to call her Fancy Nancy again. Not even when it was just her and Don.

Opening her eyes felt more complicated than it should and it took her a minute to remember why she had set the alarm in the first place. Right, for church. She had to be at church. God did not care how hungover she was.

Then again, did God really even care if she went to church or not, Joyce wondered as she pulled on her panty hose and scrubbed off the mascara that had smeared on her cheek. Probably not. At least not the God Joyce believed in, who was fairly disinterested, as higher beings went.

She still had to go to church, though, because they'd be saying a special prayer for Don and everyone else on the Covid ward. How would it look if his wife wasn't there, to look grateful and worried, but strong, and to thank everyone over and over again for their thoughts and prayers?

"I think people would understand if you missed a service, Mom," Heather had said when Joyce had complained in a moment of weakness.

"You don't know them like I do," Joyce answered.

Which was true. Heather didn't go to West Lanier anymore. When the spiritual mood struck her, which was not that often, Heather loaded the kids in the car and drove all the way to some church in Jeffersonville. A friend of Heather's sang in the church band there and after, they went to brunch at some hip restaurant across the river in Louisville. Church as an excuse for mimosas.

Heather was forever trying to get Joyce and Don to go with them, but Joyce found the idea of driving to another town to go to church horrifying. It had to be against the rules and if it wasn't, it should be.

"It's not as if you haven't changed churches before," Don had pointed out.

Joyce ignored that, as she ignored so many things. The key to a good marriage. "We will not be driving to Jeffersonville to go to church," she said. On this, she would not budge.

She took longer than usual in the bathroom to get her hair right, which made her too late to sit in her usual spot, in the pew beside Carol. Instead, she settled in at the back, which almost defeated the purpose, as no one would see her when they called Don's name. Still, God would know she was there. Joyce would know.

Her stomach growled and she thought her hair might smell of cigarette smoke or worse. Luckily, she didn't know the family in the pew beside her. She dug in her purse for a mint, but the little tin was empty. Of course it was.

The beginning notes of the next praise song jerked her awake. Falling asleep in church, like she was five years old again, sitting beside her mother. Only she hadn't fallen asleep in *her* church, had she? It had never been as boring as West Lanier, with everyone stiff and upright in their seats, lulled into a stupor by the droning voice of the preacher. At least she hadn't missed them calling Don's name. And because she was at the back, she could slip out quickly, without having to talk to anyone when the service was over. That was her hope, at least.

She was almost to the door when she heard someone calling her name.

"Oh, Joyce. How is Don doing? We're all praying for him."

Joyce knew that voice. Christine Parker. The former pastor's wife. Could she pretend she hadn't heard her? No. Christine was too close. It was too late.

"Thank you, Christine." Joyce turned and sucked down the sigh that rose in her throat. She allowed Christine to take both her hands in hers, like she always did. Christine closed her eyes and bent her head for a moment, her hands holding Joyce firmly in place. There was no telling how long it would last either, this bowed-head communion. It would last until Christine had communed with God for the satisfactory amount of time. Joyce was probably supposed to bow her own head with Christine, but she didn't have the patience for it this morning. At last, Christine raised her head and opened her eyes.

"How is Don? Have you talked to him today?" Christine did not let go of Joyce's hands.

"Well, not today," Joyce said. "It's early. He sleeps a lot." All true. All absolutely true.

"Any signs of improvement?" Christine asked.

Joyce smiled to hide her panic. Were there signs of improvement? She had no idea. Did Christine understand how hard it was to talk to the doctor? Did she realize how busy Joyce was?

"Not really," Joyce said at last. "He's still on the ventilator."

"Oh, but I heard from Lisa Joyner that they might take him off the ventilator this week." Christine tilted her head that way she did and studied Joyce.

Was that true? Joyce had "talked" to Don before the party yesterday, which meant the nurse had held the phone up to his ear while Joyce babbled and Don made long, hoarse breathing noises in response. She'd asked the nurse how he was doing but only got a cursory answer. Joyce didn't like hassling the nurses for updates that didn't exist. "He had more energy today," the nurses would say. Or, "He ate all his breakfast." What did any of it add up to?

"Yes," Joyce said at last. "That's good news at least." She swallowed hard on the burp she felt working its way up her throat, tasting of olives and gin.

Christine squeezed her hands tighter. "Oh, you poor thing. I'll come by this week. I know you must be climbing the walls with worry. I'll make my monkey bread. We'll have coffee and a good long talk."

"That would be lovely." Joyce gritted her teeth on the lie.

"I feel so grateful the Lord took John before he had to endure all this." Christine placed one hand on top of her heart, the other still holding tight to Joyce. "I pray I get to join him soon."

Joyce nodded. She used to doubt Christine when she said that sort of thing, wishing for death over and over again, but not anymore.

She'd seen the fervor shining in Christine's eyes when she talked about going home to the Lord. More power to her and her death wish. Joyce had hated Christine's husband, Brother John, the pastor at West Lanier. She was glad he was gone to the Lord too.

"Well, you take good care of yourself, Joyce." Christine squeezed Joyce's hand one last time, hard enough to make the arthritis knot on her pinky finger hurt.

"I will," Joyce said. Then she turned and was practically running out the door to her car. Her stomach felt like it wanted to float out of her body, and she couldn't tell if it was nausea or hunger. Either way, she was going home to crawl back in bed.

>>

Dr. Barrett confirmed what Christine had heard. He hoped to take Don off the ventilator sometime that week.

"And then what?" Joyce asked. "Is he out of the woods?"

"Hard to tell," Dr. Barrett said. The man had zero bedside manner. "It's certainly a step in the right direction."

"Will he be able to come home?" Joyce asked. It was Monday and she'd cleaned up all the remnants from the party except for the note someone had left on her fridge, nestled among the pictures of grandchildren and a faded list of important phone numbers. "Joyce throws a kickass party," the note said and someone had drawn a little cartoon sketch that was unmistakably her, wearing a pantsuit with a martini glass in hand. She stared at the note now and thought about how, if Don came home, the note could not stay. Of course it couldn't. She would have to burn it or hide it.

"Not ready to come home quite yet," Dr. Barrett said. "But once the ventilator is gone, we can schedule a visit for you."

"Oh, thank you." Joyce leaned against the counter and pressed her hand against her face. "Thank you."

She did think sometimes about what it must be like for Don, one long day after another in that hospital bed. Of course she did. She worried that he was lonely. She'd brought as many things from home as they'd let her. Photos. His favorite slippers. The blanket his grandmother had crocheted for them, which, good riddance. Joyce hated that blanket.

But for the first time in their marriage, she couldn't put herself inside Don's day-to-day existence. She couldn't imagine what it was like. The nurses said he slept a lot, but when he was awake? What then? Did he contemplate his own death? Did he have regrets? Would he be a different man at the end of this? Or would it be the same old Don who came home?

The visit, the nurse informed her, would last an hour and could include up to three visitors, which meant Joyce had to decide who to bring. Or maybe she would let Heather decide. Maybe she would let the children visit Don without her. Wouldn't that be a good, motherly sacrifice to make? Children were more important than wives anyway.

Joyce sat in Don's chair in their living room, staring out at the river in the distance, concentrating as hard as she could on imagining Don in his hospital room alone. This was her penance. She made herself think of Don and nothing else for at least an hour every day, but it was never all at once, which made it hard to keep track.

Of course, he was in her thoughts all the time, but this was different. This was whole body concentration. Like meditation, she guessed, which Heather talked about but Joyce had never tried.

Then a robin flitted into the tree out the window, which made her think of the backyard and the beets in her little raised bed that needed thinning, so, next thing, she was out of the chair and putting on her garden shoes. While she was out there, she might as well weed the iris bed, too, and edge around the brick border, which was usually Don's job, but if he did come home, wouldn't it make him happy to see that it was already done?

>>

The truth was, Joyce didn't want to go to the hospital to see Don. She was afraid of how he'd look. She'd seen enough on the phone during their video chats to know it wouldn't be good. She felt at times that the man in that hospital bed could not be her husband. Her husband was gone. Not dead. None of that finality. Just disappeared under mysterious circumstances.

Maybe she wouldn't even recognize Don anymore. Maybe it wasn't him, like those baby mix-ups you read about, only with a sick old man. Maybe it was all a plot Don had devised to escape his life. He'd gotten over the Covid weeks ago. Or he'd never had it in the first place. He'd hired someone else to take his place in the hospital bed. All old white men looked alike. Meanwhile, the real Don was in Arizona, in one of those senior living communities. Soaking up the sun. Golfing. Having cocktails on the sun porch with Julie Davis.

Maybe Joyce just wouldn't go to the hospital at all, only Heather arranged to pick her up, so she had no choice.

When she stepped through the door, Don was still recognizable, propped up in his hospital bed. He was sunken and pale, but still Don. An oxygen mask covered the lower half of his face. He had to take the mask off to talk, but then he started gasping, so, for once, Don Blankman had no choice but to listen.

Joyce sat where she was supposed to sit, beside his bed. His hand felt soft and formless held in hers. Had a nurse been putting lotion on him?

Don Jr. stood with his hands in his pockets, staring out the window. "It's good to see you, Dad," he kept saying. Heather ran through her list of all the awards and milestones achieved by the kids in the past three weeks. Then she, too, stuttered into silence.

"Well, we'll let you and Mom have some time alone," Don Jr. said at last, as if this was an amazing gift and not an immense relief for him to be freed from that room.

"Oh, no," Joyce started to protest, but they were already out the door, leaving her alone with Don.

>>

"Well," Joyce said into the new silence, punctuated by the beeping of all the machines Don was connected to.

She had to lean forward ever so slightly in order to hold Don's hand and she wished she could quit. It was hurting her back. She'd overdone it with the gardening. She always did in the spring, her eagerness pushing her past her body's limits.

"I edged the beds in the backyard," she said into the silence.

Don squeezed her hand in his. His other hand shook as he brought it to his face to pull the mask away.

"I'm going to be okay, Joyce," he rasped. "Don't worry."

Joyce patted his hand and set it back down on the bed. She pushed her back against the chair and tried to twist her hip into a more comfortable position. "Hard not to worry, Don, but I'll do my best."

She glanced at the window ledge, packed with flower arrangements and potted plants. Did the nurses sort through the arrangements to throw out the faded ones? Did they water the plants?

"Everyone at church has been praying for you," Joyce said. Don's eyes drooped as he struggled to stay awake. "I saw Christine. That woman doesn't seem to age, you know. God's chosen, I guess. She looks just the same as when I joined the church all those years ago."

Joyce got up and crossed to the window, glancing at the cards on the flower arrangements. "Oh, the college sent you flowers. Isn't that nice?"

Don nodded, though she doubted he was hearing her.

"You know, I still have that necklace somewhere, the one Christine gave me when I joined the church. I always wondered if she did that for everyone, but then when Heather got baptized, Brother John was already gone."

She felt the soil in the schefflera pot. Damp. Someone had watered it.

"Do you remember Heather cried and cried when they re-baptized me that Sunday at the front of the church?" Joyce said. "She was hysterical. She thought Brother John was trying to drown me. She didn't understand."

On the back of her hand, Joyce found a line of red paint, a remnant from her latest still-life stuck in the crease of a wrinkle. She didn't bother trying to wipe it off.

"I didn't want to do that, you know. Get re-baptized. I'd been saved in my parents' church since I was five years old, Don. I was holier than any of those people at West Lanier. But Brother John said it had to be three times. Three dunks. Backwards. The way they'd done it at our church didn't count. What a load of crap."

She stared at her reflection in the window, her face surrounded by the bright palette of flowers. What a painting that would make. *Old woman with halo of flowers.*

"It was humiliating. A grown woman baptized in that tank with all the children. That's what they wanted. To humiliate me. And you didn't care, Don. You went right along with it."

Joyce knew he was asleep. She wasn't going to let that stop her.

"But I did it. I left my church. Spent the next twenty years fighting to get the children out of bed and dressed and presentable every Sunday to get them to West Lanier. That's what I did."

Foot washers. That's what Don had called the people in Joyce's church. They didn't have a denomination, but she didn't know what that was, anyway, until she joined West Lanier. Foot washers. Yes, that was what they were. That was what they did. Once a month at church, they washed each other's feet. Joyce's mother had always made sure she and her sister were extra clean those Sundays. Their toenails neatly trimmed.

Don had laughed and laughed when she had told him about it. "Are you serious?" he'd said.

She'd never felt so ashamed. She'd never told the children. She had gone to West Lanier with Don and that had been that until Christine had pried the secret of her inadequate baptism out of her in Sunday school one day. It wouldn't do. She'd have to be baptized again, the *right* way. The *correct* way.

"Well, it doesn't matter now, does it?" Joyce said. She crossed to the chair and gathered her purse. Her coat. She leaned over Don and ran her fingers across his forehead, like she was painting a bold stroke across his wrinkles. His skin there was dry.

The truth was life was lonelier without the foot washing. Its absence left a blank space deep inside her. No one understood the intimacy of it. The care. Sometimes over those long years, sitting in the church pew at West Lanier, their bodies barely touching, Joyce would get flashes of memories behind her closed eyes. Her small foot cradled in a wrinkled hand, gently running the cloth they used over the soles of her feet, tickling ever so slightly. Or Mrs. Cropper's gnarled and tiny feet in Joyce's own hands, the way the old woman had closed her eyes in pleasure. "Bless you, child," Mrs. Cropper would murmur. "Bless you." And Joyce *had* felt blessed. Caring and cared for in a way she'd never felt at West Lanier.

"I miss you, Donny," Joyce whispered, just to try the words out. It felt like there might still be some truth there. She imagined telling Don the sun porch was her studio now. What objection could he possibly have? They didn't use the room for anything else. She imagined them hanging one of her paintings in the living room, opposite her chair, so that would become her view. She thought about finding a picture of the old church and painting that, a reminder of what she'd felt back then. A reminder of what she'd lost.

"Come home soon," Joyce said to the silent room.

The door opened and a nurse bustled in. "Sorry. Time's up," she said.

"Oh, that's fine," Joyce said. "I'm done." She glanced around the room to make sure everything was in its place. She patted her purse held tight against her side and smoothed the wrinkles out of her skirt. Had she forgotten anything?

No, she was good. She had everything she needed.

Return

When the pandemic was over, James decided that he was done with San Francisco. He was done with California. He was done with that whole idiotic, go-west-young-man American dream that kept getting rebooted one generation to the next. Frankly, he was embarrassed by the fact that it had ever been appealing to him in the first place.

He pulled out a map of the country he'd found tucked under the passenger seat of the 2010 Honda Civic he'd inherited from his older sister. He would do this the analog way. He was tired of a digital life. He closed his eyes. He spun around once for good measure in the tiny apartment he shared with three other people slowly giving up on their own California dreams. He bumped into one of his roommate's wall of dying plants, which they did not have room for. He hovered his finger over the map and then pushed it down so hard his knuckle popped.

"Fuck," he muttered, at the knuckle and the spot he'd landed on. Texas. No way he was going there.

"What are you doing?" one of the roommates called from behind the sheet that turned part of the dining room into an extra bedroom.

James ignored him. He tried again, minus the spinning. Connecticut. Bleh. Montana. He pictured cowboys and dust. Definitely not.

He left the map where it was and pulled out his phone. He Googled "the opposite of San Francisco." He Googled "most boring town in the Midwest." He Googled "when will things get better instead of worse already?" He took a nap. Got up. He texted his mom, "What was the name of that town where Grandpa Joe lived?" He Googled, "Lanier, Indiana."

Three days later, his car was packed and he was headed east, the direction of return.

>>

Grandpa Joe had died while James was still in college, majoring in theater, which Grandpa Joe had made no secret of telling him was no career for a real man. James knew that, of course. He'd minored in computer science, but he hadn't wanted to hang out with those people. That's what the theater major was for—to provide an acceptable social life.

They had sold Grandpa Joe's house after he died, but James's mom called some of Grandpa Joe's friends in Lanier, and one of them, a dude named Dr. Harvey, offered for James to stay rent-free in what he called "the shack." in exchange for mowing the lawns at all the other properties Dr. Harvey owned.

"But, Mom, how expensive could rent be in Lanier?" James had asked when his mother had told him this arrangement.

"More expensive than you think," his mother said.

James didn't believe her. It was Lanier, Indiana. No one wanted to live there. Well, James wanted to live there, but he was unique. He was swimming upstream. He was breaking the pattern.

As he drove across Nebraska and Missouri, he imagined what Dr. Harvey's shack might look like. In his head, it was a little like the house where Thoreau had lived, though then James had to admit to himself that he had no idea what Thoreau's house had looked like. He told himself he'd look it up at the next rest stop, but then he forgot.

At any rate, when James got to Lanier, he discovered Dr. Harvey's "shack" was not a shack at all but a small, ranch-style house that sat in the alley behind Dr. Harvey's row of new condos.

"Not much of a view, I'm afraid," Dr. Harvey said as he gave James the tour.

The shack had a kitchen and a bathroom. Wi-Fi and a big-screen TV, plus a brand-new gaming system. The gaming system was for Dr. Harvey's nephews, he explained. The shack was surrounded on all sides by similar small, ranch-style houses. Most of the windows looked directly into other windows. James may not have ever seen Thoreau's house, but he knew that this was not what it had looked like. There had certainly not been an Xbox.

Dr. Harvey gave James instructions on how to access the Wi-Fi and when to take the trash out and where to set the thermostat.

"I'd take you out to dinner, but I've got a date with my new girl-friend," Dr. Harvey said. He stood in the doorway of the shack, practically bouncing with anticipation.

Gross, James thought. Dr. Harvey was old.

"Call if you need anything," Dr. Harvey said.

>>

James resisted the pull of the Xbox and went out to explore his new hometown. He figured it wouldn't take long.

Lanier looked exactly the way he remembered it. Nothing had changed. His family hadn't visited Grandpa Joe a lot when James was little, but every time, it had felt like one of those magical adven-tures from the children's books he'd never finished because he knew they'd have to leave the magical place in the end and go back to the real world, and he hated that part. Grandpa Joe's house had been like a Hollywood mansion or a haunted house, full of staircases in strange places and stairs that creaked and floors that sloped so that when James dropped a marble on one side of the dining room, it would roll slowly all the way into the kitchen, a trick that never got old.

James walked past Grandpa Joe's house on Main Street and wondered who lived there now. He wondered if the people would let him go inside. He wondered if the floors still sloped.

He would stop and see one day, but first he needed food. He tapped the battered copy of *Walden* he'd bought at a used bookstore somewhere in Wyoming against his leg as he wandered up and down Main Street. A woman in a bright-pink tracksuit rode by on a pink bicycle, slow and steady down the street, her long hair wafting out behind her. Okay, he hadn't remembered that from his other visits.

There were more restaurants than he remembered, too, but he wasn't interested in those. He headed straight for the bar he'd always wanted to go inside when he was little. It had booths set in the windows and was always crowded. James remembered the sound of music wafting out along with the scent of greasy food, but he'd always been too young to eat there.

Now he opened the door and marched up to the bar, setting his book on the wooden surface and glancing around.

"I just drove across the country from San Francisco," he wanted to announce to everyone in the bar. He wasn't sure why.

He stared up at the list of beers on tap that flashed on the TV screen. There were a lot of beers and, yes, they were cheaper than in San Francisco, but not that much cheaper, and he didn't have a job yet or much savings. No one could save any money living in San Francisco. Would he be able to here? And what would he be saving the money for? Whatever. He didn't have to figure that out now. There was time.

"You know, he wasn't really all that isolated." The bartender slapped a coaster down in front of James and pointed at his book. She was middle-aged, thick-ish, with a T-shirt that said "St. Petersburg, Florida—Heaven's Waiting Room." The T-shirt was mildly interesting, except for the Florida part, which everyone knew was the stupidest state in the whole stupid country.

"Railroad tracks ran right by his house and people were visiting him all the time," the bartender said.

"What?" James looked behind him, not sure if the bartender was talking to him or not. Nothing she was saying made sense.

"Thoreau." She tapped her finger on his book. "It wasn't like he was in the wilderness or anything when he wrote that."

"Of course," James said. He had not known this and even now, he hoped that the bartender was making it up. "I knew that."

"Still a good read though," the bartender said.

"Yeah, I read it once a year," James said. This was a lie. He'd never read all of *Walden*. He imagined that he had to have read parts of it at some point, even if he couldn't remember any actual specifics. He'd talked about it in a class once, at least. That was true.

"What can I get you?" the bartender asked.

"Do you have any smoked beers?" James asked.

"Did you say 'smoked'?"

"Yeah, *smoked*."

The bartender stared at him, the corner of her lip pulled up into the tiniest smile.

"There's a whole bar that specializes in smoked beers in San Francisco," James said.

"Is there?" Her lips twitched, the beginnings of a smirk. She nodded. "Well, no smoked beers here, sadly. So."

She did not ask him if he was from San Francisco. She did

not seem particularly interested in learning more about smoked beers.

James sighed and settled for a hazy IPA, mostly so the bartender would go away. He started to open *Walden*, but he didn't want the bartender to see he was only on page 4. Also, *Walden* was boring.

Instead, he pulled out the Moleskine notebook he'd bought at the same bookstore where he'd picked up the Thoreau. He wasn't sure what he would do with the notebook at the time, but it seemed an important prop to have. He had to borrow a pen from the bartender, earning another smirk. He began to try to figure out, projecting from the cost of this beer, how long his money would last. The prospects were not good, and he had moved on to composing a text to his mother to ask for a loan—the kind that would never be repaid—when he felt a tap on his shoulder.

He turned around to see an older woman, with short hair and glasses funky enough even for San Francisco. She wore a chunky necklace that looked like it was made of scrap metal and a shirt that could pass for either a famous abstract painting or a very bad art project by a toddler.

"Oh, oh." The woman tapped a finger against her lower lip. "You must be the *writer*."

James looked at the notebook and his non-smoked beer. He looked at his dismal financial prospects laid out on the page in front of him. He saw the bartender woman smirking at him from the end of the bar.

"Yeah. The writer," James said. "That's me."

And that was how it began.

>>

Before he really knew what had happened, James found himself sitting at a table with three middle-aged women who were all very excited to meet the-writer-who-had-just-moved-to-Lanier, as Pam introduced him. Pam was the woman who'd tapped him on the shoulder, with the funky glasses and the scrap-metal necklace. She told him the other two women's names, but James had already forgotten them.

He exchanged numbers with one of the women, who ran some sort of art organization in town. She promised they'd talk soon, though James hoped not. Pam was on the library board and would get in touch with the director about James doing an event. Maybe a workshop for the kids. The other woman at the table would make sure James got interviewed by the local newspaper.

"It'll be great for your brand," she assured him.

Their food had come and James was taking his first bite of the Saloon Burger when it occurred to him that there was a real writer out there somewhere whom he was now impersonating. A real writer he knew nothing about and now couldn't find out about, because he could hardly ask the women questions about himself that he was already supposed to know.

Then again, he thought as he popped a tater tot in his mouth, who could really prove one way or the other if he was a writer or not?

"What's your book *called*?" Pam asked.

James bought himself time by taking another bite of his burger. He knew from his aspiring-writer roommate back in San Francisco, the one trying to follow in the footsteps of Kerouac, that the process of publishing a book was slippery and byzantine. No one understood how it worked, and he could use that to his advantage.

"Oh, my book's out on submission," he said. "And, you know, the publisher will decide on the title, so what does it matter what I call it?"

Pam nodded knowingly, even though James was certain she had no idea what he was talking about.

When the rest of the women peppered him with questions about genre or where he got his ideas, he changed the subject, which worked like a charm. The truth was, no one wanted to actually read the book someone had (or in James's case, *hadn't*) written. They just wanted to say they knew a writer.

No, truly, James considered, his only concern was that the real writer would surface. Who were they and what did Pam know about them? This was what James needed to find out, but how?

It was a small inconvenience, nothing James couldn't handle, and on the plus side, Pam picked up his tab, so maybe the whole writer thing could work.

>>

By the time he finished saying good-bye to the table of women, a process that took almost as long as the meal itself, James was exhausted. He went back to the shack and collapsed onto the lumpy bed. He awoke the next morning to a knock on the door.

"No," he groaned, only half awake.

He sprang upright at the sound of a key turning in the lock and the front door opening.

"I don't have anything to steal!" James shouted. This was what he and his roommates back in San Francisco had agreed on as the best strategy for dealing with a possible break-in, though they'd thankfully never had the chance to try it out.

"I know you don't." Dr. Harvey knocked once on the door frame that led into the bedroom and then walked in. "How's the bed?"

"Fine." James pulled the sheets up to cover his bare chest and then let them drop. What did he care what this old dude thought of him? "What are you doing here?"

"Forgot to give you the key to the shed for the mower." Dr. Harvey opened the closet door and glanced inside. "So, I hear you're famous."

"What?" James picked up his cell phone and stared at the screen, waiting for it to explain what the hell was happening to him right now.

"One night in Lanier and everyone's talking about you," Dr. Harvey said.

James couldn't tell by the expression on Dr. Harvey's face if he was joking or not. He couldn't decide which would be better.

"You didn't tell me you were a writer," Dr. Harvey said.

"Well, it's not like I'm famous or something." James laughed.

"You are now."

"No, it was just that one woman in the bar."

Dr. Harvey snorted. "It's never just one woman in a bar."

"It's not a big deal." James tossed his phone back onto the dresser. It was no help. He wished Dr. Harvey would leave already.

"Hmm." Dr. Harvey stuck his hands deep into the pockets of his corduroy pants and jingled his change. The dude actually had change in his pockets. "Because you're Joe's grandson, I'm going to give you some advice." He lifted his eyebrows and stared at James. "Are you listening?"

"Yeah." Who *was* this guy?

"In a town like Lanier, small actions have big consequences," Dr. Harvey said.

"Okay." James didn't know what that meant. He also didn't care.

"Tread lightly," Dr. Harvey said.

"Right." Would he leave now?

Dr. Harvey watched James for what felt like an eternity. He sighed. "This should get interesting," he mumbled as he turned and walked out the door.

James heard a key plink onto the kitchen counter and then the front door closed.

>>

"James, would you like another Manhattan?"

James glanced down at his drink, which, sure enough, was almost empty. How many Manhattans was that now? It was hard to keep track. He'd been sitting on Pam's patio for hours and the drinks kept appearing in his hand.

"Well —," he started.

"Oh, oh, one more *won't* hurt." Pam waved her hand at her husband. James had forgotten his name. "Get James another *Manhattan*," she commanded, and the husband dutifully got up and trotted into the kitchen.

Pam talked weird in a way James could not quite put his finger on. Maybe it was because she was always commanding people to do something. Pam did a lot of commanding. And a lot of drinking. Everyone he'd met in Lanier seemed to do a lot of drinking, enough to put James to shame. These old people could *drink*, and old people were pretty much all James had met, starting with Pam and moving out from there.

"You're not the only *person* to move here from California," Pam had said to him. "It's just most of *them* are in their seventies."

If there were young people in Lanier, James hadn't seen them, let alone met them. Anyway, it was cool to be one of the few young people in town, like he was ahead of schedule.

"Will you set your next book in Lanier?" a woman at the table next to James's asked. "It would be such a unique location, don't you think?"

James nodded. He didn't trust himself to speak without slurring.

They were sitting on Pam's patio, an elaborate garden tucked between Pam's house and the one next door. Her garden was nothing like the suburban yards James had grown up with. It was nothing like any garden he'd seen, apart from the "after" segments on the home-makeover shows one of his roommates sometimes watched while he got high. Every house he'd been to in Lanier so far looked like the "after" scene in a reality-TV show.

James did not remember people being this rich in Lanier when he used to visit Grandpa Joe. Granted, he hadn't gone inside any houses besides Grandpa Joe's and that one had definitely been the "before" version of the home-makeover show. His grandfather's house had been all sagging La-Z-Boy recliner and shag carpet in the bedrooms. The back yard had been small, with patchy grass that Grandma was always yelling at Grandpa Joe to mow before the neighbors complained. James hadn't minded any of that.

He imagined Grandpa Joe's house and yard looked very different now. Pam had told him who lived in Grandpa Joe's house—people from Chicago who came here a few weekends a year—and even offered to introduce him. That would mean another patio and more heavy drinking and James wasn't sure if his liver could survive.

"You don't have to drink it, you know."

James turned to the woman sitting beside him. If he moved too quickly, everything would start spinning. He didn't think this was the same woman who'd been sitting there when he had first sat down, but it was hard to know for sure. She might have told him her name.

Natalie? Nancy? Naomi? It was hard for him to imagine a woman this old named Naomi, but what did he know?

The woman nodded at the full glass that had appeared in front of him. "You don't have to drink it. Tony will keep making them, but that doesn't mean you have to drink them."

"But wouldn't that be rude?" James spoke each word slowly and hoped he didn't sound as drunk as he felt.

"Spoken like a true Midwesterner," the woman said. "I thought you were from California."

"I grew up in Ohio." James suppressed a hiccup, which came out sounding like a high-pitched chirp.

"Ah." The woman pulled the lime garnish off her drink and tossed it into the landscaping behind her. "How do you like the shack?"

James squeezed his eyes shut, as if this might reset the conversation. And the evening. As if it might reset the last week of his life. He shouldn't have been surprised that this woman knew where he lived at this point. He didn't even know her name. "What is up with this place?" he whispered. "Does everyone know my Social Security number, too?"

"No, not that." The woman shrugged. "But there's a good chance they know what you ate for breakfast and what time you get up in the morning."

"It's like I'm famous," James whispered. He wasn't sure why.

"You are," the woman said.

"I don't like it."

"No. Why would you?"

He pushed his Manhattan away from him across the table. "How do I make it stop?"

"Move away?"

James felt his eyes droop. He pictured the silence of the shack. "I don't have anywhere to go. I don't know what I'm doing. I don't know why I'm even here in the first place."

"Yeah, join the crowd," the woman said. "I'm eighty-one and I still haven't figured any of that shit out."

"Oh, oh," he could hear Pam say from somewhere on the patio, her voice moving closer.

"I need help," James said. He looked at the woman beside him. She was like a much better version of his grandmother. Her hair was still stylish. Her eyes still bright. Still alive in a way his grandmother had never seemed to be.

He thought maybe he wanted to lean over and hug the woman. He thought that she would be okay with it. Everyone he'd met in Lanier was big on hugging. Sometimes they'd even do the thing where they kissed him on the cheek, which he thought was something no one did except in old movies. Not even the French, anymore. The pandemic had almost killed them all. Surely extraneous kissing should no longer occur. And yet, in Lanier, it was all the rage.

But this woman he wanted to hug. He wanted to tell her that he was not, in fact, the writer, though he had started to question even this truth. Maybe if all these people believed he was the writer, he was. He had a notebook, after all, even if there was still nothing written in it. He still went to that bar some afternoons, usually when he knew the smirking bartender would not be working. He took his copy of *Walden*, which he still had probably not read. He thought that was something a writer would probably do.

He wanted to tell this woman that he was starting to think that all the drinking was interfering with his antidepressants. Or maybe it was the vertigo of moving. Or the stress of pretending to be someone he was not. Maybe it was all of the above that made him feel wrong, as if he'd come to a dead-end and there was no way out.

He wanted to tell this woman that he was ignoring his mother's calls and he wasn't sure why, and she was threatening to drive down from Columbus and see what was going on.

"I need help," James said again. "Can you help me?"

"Absolutely, honey." The woman laid her wrinkled hand on top of James's. "But right now, I have to scoot, because Pam is headed this way."

She pulled herself up out of the chair and stepped into the land-scaping, disappearing behind a big clump of purple flowers. James wondered if maybe she'd never been there at all.

"Oh, oh." Pam slid herself into the empty chair beside James. "There's a reading next *week* at the coffee shop. You have to *read* from your novel. You *simply* must."

>>

When James had agreed to do lawn care in exchange for rent, Dr. Harvey had not bothered to explain how many properties he owned or where they were. James had imagined other houses downtown, like the shack, which had a yard that took less than three minutes to mow and trim. Most of the time would be taken up with getting the mower started. Taking care of a few other yards like that would be no big deal.

Then Dr. Harvey presented James with the list of properties, which was several pages long.

"You can't be serious," James said as he flipped the page over. He started to count the number of addresses and then stopped.

"Do you know how much I could get for this place if I rented it out as an AirBnB?" Dr. Harvey said. He was wearing corduroy again, even though it was warm outside.

"There aren't any AirBnBs in Lanier," James said. Who would stay here? Who besides him, but he was different.

"There are over a hundred AirBnBs in Lanier, in fact." Dr. Harvey ran his thumb over a chip in the paint on the trim around the kitchen door.

"I didn't do that," James thought to say, but would that make him sound guilty?

"It's a problem, really, all the shotgun houses being converted to AirBnBs," Dr. Harvey said. "No place for young people to live anymore. Or old people who aren't loaded like me."

This was all familiar to James from conversations he'd heard in San Francisco. He was skeptical that Lanier could be facing the same problem.

"Let me show you how to load the mower onto the trailer," Dr. Harvey said.

This was not a skill James wanted to learn, but Dr. Harvey went through it several times before making James do it himself.

"I made a schedule for you. Page four." Dr. Harvey nodded toward the stack of papers that James had left on the front porch. "Stick to it."

Or what?, James thought. Would Dr. Harvey kick him out? It seemed unlikely.

He didn't want to push it though, so on a Thursday afternoon, he loaded up the mower and headed to the first property on the list.

"Fuck me," he said as he pulled up. The yard was huge and all he had was a push mower. This was going to take forever.

He put in his AirPods and started a podcast that was two guys talking about how stupid everything was in a way that James had once found funny and interesting. After several yanks on the pull cord, which threatened to dislocate his shoulder, he got the mower going.

As he trudged back and forth across the lawn, he thought about the writer, lurking somewhere in Lanier. The writer, he imagined, was not mowing lawns. The writer was probably staying someplace much nicer than the shack. The writer did not have a landlord who gave one quick warning knock before he used his key to come into the apartment.

Had the writer heard of James? Did the writer realize his identity had been stolen? Could the writer hold his liquor better than James, who had on more than one occasion since he had arrived in Lanier found himself sweating away the night on the bathroom floor in the shack? How did the old people do it night after night? James had more than once considered asking them if there was some secret to heavy drinking they'd discovered in their long lives that they now refused to share.

When he got to the second property, he didn't bother with the AirPods or the podcast. He surrendered to the white noise of the mower. There was a mindlessness to the process that wasn't the worst thing.

It was late afternoon by the time he'd gotten halfway through the list. He turned off the mower and pulled the edge of his T-shirt up to wipe the sweat off his face. With the mower off, the silence was louder. Insistent.

He grabbed one of the energy drinks he'd bought at a gas station. It was warm now but he guzzled it down anyway. He'd have to start bringing water, like in high school when he was in the marching band. He wondered if Mom still had that big thermos they'd all had to buy and pack with ice water early every morning before heading up to the high school parking lot for band camp. In August. In southern Ohio. In retrospect, it had all been a lawsuit waiting to happen.

His legs shook a little as he sat on the edge of the trailer. He wiped at the sweat again and stared into the distance.

This property was in Kentucky, on the other side of the river from Lanier. On the map on his phone, he could see he'd been following a river on the long drive to get there. He couldn't see the river from where he sat now, but the lush green walls of the valley lurked in the distance. They were a bright green that did battle with the late afternoon haze. He'd passed hardly any cars on the twisting road that led to this house and none had come by as he sat there. If anyone lived in the house behind him, they weren't there now.

James finished off the last of the energy drink and lay back in the trailer. It was so quiet here. The loudest thing was the sound of the insects. The hills were covered in trees, but they stopped in the flatland, where green fields stretched. James couldn't identify what crops were planted there. High above the valley, a bird circled and James imagined what it would be like, to see the world from those heights.

Maybe he could stay here forever, in this valley. In the house behind him. Maybe Dr. Harvey would rent it to him, even though he had no idea how he would pay. He could live here like Thoreau should have lived, not like the bartender lady said he had. He could grow a beard. Well, he couldn't actually, because his facial hair would not cooperate, but he could certainly stop shaving.

In this quiet, the answers would come. Or the questions. This was where he should be.

James closed his eyes and began to drift.

"You missed a spot."

His whole body jerked, his elbow banging against a board that stuck up in the trailer bed. He sat up, and at first he saw nothing. *Great, now I'm hearing voices*, he thought.

"The girl never missed a spot. She was better."

James leaned over the side of the trailer to see a small child standing in the driveway, pointing at a spot of tall grass that, sure enough, James had managed to miss.

"It's not that hard, you know. The mowing." The kid kicked at the gravel in the driveway. "I could do it except I can't pull hard enough to start the crappy old mower and Dr. Harvey says I'd cut my arm off." The kid squinted up at James. "I wouldn't though."

James glanced back at the house. It looked exactly the same as it had before. Abandoned. Neglected, at the very least.

"Do you live here?" he asked the kid.

"How much does Dr. Harvey pay you?" the kid asked. James thought the kid was a boy, but he couldn't be sure. The hair was long enough to go either way. The kid wore cut-off shorts and a T-shirt that read "Port William Redbirds," which was neither a place nor a team James had ever heard of.

"Where are your parents?" James asked.

"If it's less than twelve dollars an hour, he's paying you less than he paid the girl," the kid said.

"Okay." James was the youngest of three. He had no idea how to talk to small children.

"And she did a better job than you."

"That's sort of a rude thing to say, isn't it?" James brushed grass clippings off his bare arm. He pushed himself up off the trailer and stood looking down at the kid, looming over the kid, really, which felt better.

"But it's true and it's wrong to tell a lie." The kid kicked at the trailer tire, which James had to admit was also sort of rude.

"Valid point." James slicked his sweaty hair back off his fore-head. He'd realized halfway into the first lawn that he hadn't dressed appropriately for the job, in his shorts and T-shirt. It had never occurred to him to wonder why people who worked landscaping jobs always wore long pants and long-sleeved shirts. Now that his legs and arms were plastered with grass clippings and crisscrossed with scratches from where rocks and other debris had been thrown up, it all made sense.

The point was, he'd left the house looking at least passably cool and now he was a mess. Which had been fine when it was just him and the quiet, but less okay now that he faced this annoying kid.

"So you want to mow lawns?" James asked. He'd never had that easy manner he'd seen in other people, of interacting with kids. But how hard could it be?

"Of course not, not for a living." The kid gave James a pointed look, which was something James had never realized kids could do. "That would be stupid. I'd do it just for the summer."

"Right." James glanced at his smartwatch, as if he had any place to be besides drinking on the patio with a bunch of old people.

"I'm trying to make enough money to run away," the kid said.

"Oh, yeah?" James squinted at the house's windows, hoping to see someone's face peering out, keeping an eye on the kid. Nothing. "Where are you going to run away to?"

"Bermuda," the kid said.

James laughed. He couldn't help it. "Bermuda?"

"You got a better idea?" the kid said.

Not really, James thought. He'd run away to Lanier, Indiana, and that, he was beginning to see, was pathetic. Why not Bermuda? Maybe the two of them could go together.

"Well, good luck." James walked over to where the lawn mower sat, cooling down. The trailer had a ramp he could pull out and use to roll the mower up onto the bed, but it took too much effort. James had taken instead to just lifting it up, which was not helping his aching muscles or the state of his clothes.

"You're not gonna get that spot you missed?" The kid pointed again at the patch of tall grass.

"It'll be our secret." James grunted and lifted the mower up onto the trailer.

"It's hardly a secret," the kid said. "Everyone can see."

James started strapping the mower down onto the trailer. He was not going to get into an argument with this kid. "It's just a little grass, bro."

The kid didn't answer but went on staring at the patch of tall grass as James struggled with the last strap. He was putting the gas can in the back seat when the kid finally spoke again.

"Everyone said things would get better after the pandemic ended, but they lied." The kid's voice was barely a whisper in all that quiet.

James was about to slam the back door shut, but he stopped.

The words were a punch to his gut. He wrapped an arm around his stomach and leaned against the door. He stared at the kid, framed in the open truck window.

"Fuck, kid," he whispered.

The kid was right. Of course, the kid was right. It didn't matter who "everyone" was. The kid's parents or teachers or the people on TV. Maybe no one had to make the promise at all. It had just been there in the air they breathed.

On the other side of this shitshow, things would be better. That had been the promise. It had felt like a promise to James. Of course it had felt like a promise to the kid. But the kid was right. It was a lie. It was all a lie. Nothing was better. Nothing was ever going to be better.

"At least in Bermuda there's a beach." The kid stared at James, one hand picking at the frayed end of their jean shorts. "I've never been to the beach."

"It's nice," James said.

Of course at the beaches close to San Francisco, the water was too cold to swim. The waves were too high. The beaches too rocky and covered with sea lions or seals that scared the crap out of James with their big bodies and lack of coordination. But during the pandemic, one of the roommates would drive them out to the beach sometimes. They'd all peel off their masks when they reached that windy expanse, like they were breathing again for the first time.

James had stood and stared out at the ocean and imagined Japan or whatever was on the other side and he'd thought, *This is still here.* The ocean was still there. There was only so much humans were capable of fucking up. Yeah, sure the ocean was full of plastic and too warm and everything in it was dying. But it was still there. Knowing that had felt okay. The most okay he'd felt in those pandemic years.

James thought about trying to comfort the kid, but he couldn't think of a way to do it that didn't involve more lies.

"I hope you get to Bermuda," he said. "I'll put in a good word for you with Dr. Harvey."

"Thanks," the kid said.

The kid moved away from the car and the trailer and stood in the driveway as James pulled out and drove away. The kid didn't wave, just stood there and watched. James got the strange sense that the kid would always be there, in the same spot in that valley. The kid would never make it to Bermuda. The kid would grow old standing right there in that driveway and there was nothing anyone could do about it.

Dr. Harvey's mowing schedule was punishing, which meant James was back at that little house the next week to mow the grass again. The spot he'd missed had been cut in a haphazard way, like someone had hacked away at it with scissors. James imagined the kid out there in the yard doing just that.

He went back to that house again and again over the next few months, but the kid never reappeared. He went early in the morning, when the valley was full of mist and Dr. Harvey's mower groaned over the grass wet with dew. He went right before the sun disappeared over the gentle hills and the fields were filled with fire-flies. Still, the kid did not appear. The house looked as abandoned as it ever had. Maybe the kid had never been there in the first place and it was all a hungover hallucination. James spent more time than he wanted to thinking about that kid and what might have happened. He imagined the kid in Bermuda, but he knew that was the unlike-liest of outcomes.

>>

James had more time for the mowing because the invites to parties began to disappear. He went from attending a gathering five nights a week to three. After a couple of months, he was lucky if he heard from Pam once a week.

It was annoying that the old people had suddenly decided to cut him out of their daily round of drinking. It wasn't like James had become less cool or anything. He wasn't in San Francisco anymore, but he still knew stuff, like what TikTok was.

At the same time, James had to admit that no longer being drunk five nights a week wasn't the worst thing. He called his mother and reassured her that he was okay. He went to visit Savannah, a dis-tant friend from college who lived in Louisville, and that was nice, if expensive. James tried to explain his life in Lanier to her—the free housing and the old people with their excellent drinks and food. He told her the story about how he'd been mistaken for a writer, but she didn't laugh like James thought she would.

"I get it," Savannah said. "I feel the urge to just go hide out some-where sometimes too."

"No, it's not like that," James wanted to say. But there was no point. Savannah didn't get it. No one did.

Dr. Harvey asked him to dinner and James didn't have anything else on his social calendar, so he peeled himself off the couch and washed off the orange dust from the bag of Cheetos he'd consumed and walked down to the condo by the river where Dr. Harvey lived.

Dr. Harvey was in his kitchen, wearing an apron and stirring something in a pot. He pointed James toward the deck, where he found the woman from Pam's porch—the one who'd disappeared into the landscaping after telling James he didn't have to drink his Manhattan.

"Hey, kid," she said as James sat down and stared out at the river below him. "How's life in the shack?"

"Okay," James said. He looked around, but there were no cock-tails on offer. Just a bowl of some puffed snack he couldn't identify. He picked one up and puzzled over it for a moment.

"Pork rinds," the woman said. "Delicious."

Her name was Nancy and it turned out she was Dr. Harvey's girl-friend. James still thought it was a little gross for old people to have girlfriends, but he kept that to himself. There were no cocktails. Just some white wine to go with the risotto Dr. Harvey had made.

They ate and then had fancy espressos from Dr. Harvey's new machine, and Nancy asked James questions. She asked about San Fran-cisco and why he'd come to Lanier and how he was doing. She didn't mention his writing or his books. Maybe she wasn't interested in that.

The questions made James feel exposed. He didn't know all the answers. What *was* he doing in Lanier? But in the soft light of the evening, the sun setting and only their silhouettes visible in the candlelight, it felt safe to speak into all the things he didn't know. Dr. Harvey held Nancy's hand under the table and James found himself wondering what that would feel like, to hold someone's hand like it was no big deal.

"You should meet my grandson," Nancy said as the last rays of the sun disappeared. "He's about your age. A good kid even though he needs to get the hell out of Lanier for a while." She patted James's hand. "No offense, kid."

James added her grandson's number to his contacts, even though he doubted he'd ever text him. He wouldn't have anything in common with some kid from Lanier.

Dr. Harvey gathered up the dishes and disappeared inside, leaving James alone with Nancy. He sat and watched the flicker of the candle flame in silence.

"Do you know anything about a writer who lives in Lanier?" he asked.

One half of Nancy's face was lit up by the light coming through the patio door and the other half was dark. It made it hard to make out her expression and James didn't try.

"Hmm," she said. "We've had actresses and musicians and governors. Don't know about a writer."

"No, I mean *now*," James said. "A writer who lives here now. They just moved here about the same time I came."

Nancy turned so her whole face was in the dark. "I might have heard something about that."

"Who was it? Are they still here?"

Inside, Dr. Harvey's shadow passed in front of the window and then disappeared.

"I don't know," Nancy said. "Everyone gets so excited when someone new moves to Lanier. Someone they think is important or interesting or famous." She waved her hand in the air, as if batting this all away, out into the dark, down toward the river below. "Can't lie. It gets old after a while. I mean, aren't we enough?"

"So it's all made up," James said. He wasn't interested in the social dynamics of the place. He wanted to know about the writer. "There was no writer?"

"There's Rachel at the Saloon." Nancy turned her face again. She took a sip of wine. "She put one of her stories up on her blog. I liked it."

"The *bartender*?" James pictured the woman. Her T-shirt. Her smirk. Her knowledge of Thoreau.

"Yeah, the bartender," Nancy said. "She's doing a reading this month. At the coffee shop."

James laughed. Once he started, he couldn't stop. He laughed until his eyes ran with tears. Maybe that was the point.

"Oh, honey." Nancy leaned toward him. She took his hand in hers. "It's so hard, isn't it?"

James held tight to her wrinkled, papery skin. "It is," he said. "It really is."

The Riverboat Nymphs

What the town folk knew for sure: the women came up from the river like nymphs, in the heat of an August afternoon, their shadows stretched out long behind them, black against the white sidewalk pavement. Their outlines shivered in the glare, as if at any moment they might slide out of this reality and disappear altogether.

The older woman wore a sleeveless green dress that rippled as she walked. The younger woman was in black cutoff shorts and a black halter top and black-dyed hair. They both wore identical necklaces with a red square pendant and, later, the town folk would wonder what those pendants signified. Liz thought something Wiccan. Rachel imagined a cult, though not the creepy kind. Joyce Blankman intuited more sinister meanings, but maybe none of them were right. Maybe they were just necklaces they'd bought together, mother and daughter, at a different stop along their riverboat journey, in another town downstream.

Even if it hadn't been the day of the riverboat visit, there was no mistaking that the women weren't from Lanier. It was their clothes and their hair that made them stick out, but also the languorous way they moved up the street, like conquerors inspecting their spoils.

"Like Cleopatra," Tom whispered when he told Loretta the story later. "The Elizabeth Taylor version, only better. *Cattier.*"

The rest of the riverboat people that day came up from the river in golfcarts they rented or on the large tour bus that followed *The*

American Empress as it meandered its way from New Orleans to Pitts-burgh. It was only three blocks from the river to Main Street, but it was all uphill and August and most of the riverboat people were old or frail or generally unused to walking.

The mother and daughter were unbothered by the heat. Some people said they didn't sweat at all. Some said they left puddles at their feet, as if they were river water trapped in human shapes.

What the town folk knew for sure: the women came up Wash-ington Street, passing the courthouse and the big maple tree, its leaves rustling as if they'd brought their own breeze. They asked Nancy, who was coming back from the Dollar General, where they should eat lunch. Nancy readjusted the grip on her bag of pork rinds, her guiltiest pleasure. She wasn't intimidated by the women. She'd swum naked in the Black Sea, after all.

"The Main Street Saloon, if you want booze with your lunch." Nancy winked. "And why wouldn't you?"

At the Saloon, the women ordered Sazeracs, and Rachel started to look up the recipe in her little red bartender's guide. The daughter leaned over the bar, her cleavage shallow and pale, and whispered to Rachel, "Don't bother with that. We'll tell you what to do."

Rachel swallowed hard and tried not to stare into the shadows that appeared where the daughter's shirt gaped open.

"We've been drinking Sazeracs all the way from New Orleans," the mother said.

"Oh, but what do people drink *here*?" The daughter sat back down on her stool and Rachel breathed a sigh of relief. "What's the signa-ture drink of Indiana?"

Rachel blinked and smiled. She was dazzled by the riverboat nymphs. She already knew how to make a Sazerac. She'd made them many times before. But something about the warm smell that came off the skin of the mother and daughter made her brain go fuzzy.

"I don't think we have a signature drink, really." Rachel flipped through the pages of the little red book. She was reluctant to set it down. It felt safer to have it in her hands.

"That's fine. Just a Sazerac then." The mother touched the red square at her throat, like she was casting a spell. Not just on Rachel but on the whole of the town.

This is what they knew: at the Saloon, the nymphs had the cauliflower bites, half with the honey teriyaki sauce and half with spicy buffalo. They declared them delicious. They nodded sagely after their first sip of Rachel's Sazerac, as if great secrets had been revealed. Rachel wanted desperately to know what they might be.

They paid with cash, no chance to glimpse their names on a credit card. They drifted down the street toward the flea market. They floated through the aisles crowded with discarded slow cookers and old Indiana license plates. They stopped at the corner for a moment to admire a woman in a frilly, bright-pink dress ride by on a pink bicycle. Their half smiles never wavered.

They bought hopped grapefruit bitters at one store and a pair of socks that said "Fuck off, I'm reading" at another.

They paused in front of the Blue Door, an event space nestled on Main Street between a hair salon and a bank. They stood at the windows for a long moment. Charlie saw them there and did a double take as he drove home from the college. The old man who ran the shoe store and wore a kilt every day said they stood there for ten minutes at least, but no one was sure whether to believe him or not.

At length, the riverboat nymphs glanced at each other and nodded. They passed through The Blue Door and stepped inside.

>>

The late August light slanted into the depths of the room and made the bourbon in Don Blankman's glass glow like a beacon. It should've attracted some attention, but Joyce didn't even glance his way. Only little Bethany stopped as she ran by to pat Don on his hand.

"Happy birthday, Grandpa Don!" she yelled before taking off again, running wild with a herd of children and not a one of their parents paying the least bit of attention.

"Not my birthday," Don shouted after her, but she was already gone.

Don's birthday was still months away. The party was to celebrate his new lung, though this was not how Don Blankman would have chosen to mark the occasion. It was worth celebrating, no doubt about that. He'd been through it. First the Covid that had put him in the hospital for two months in 2021, then the flu that sent him back again this year. It'd been a long road, but with his new lung, Joyce had declared he was on the other side and he might as well have a party.

Only, it was not his party. This was the realization he came to as he sat at one of the tables inside the Blue Door, watching his wife, Joyce, gossip with the bartender. This was not his celebration at all. It was Joyce's.

"Well, I guess she earned it," Don mumbled. There was no one else sitting at the table with Don. It was reserved for family, like they were at a goddamn wedding. Heather's kids were hopping on and off the stage, Bethany, the youngest, about to fall and bust her tiny head open any minute, but if no one else cared, Don didn't either. And Don Jr. was never on time, which was his wife's fault, because Don and Joyce had certainly not raised him that way.

So this party wasn't really his. So his run for school board had never gotten off the ground. So the vice at the junior high went on unchecked and he had never figured out where that sex survey had come from. So a mere cold had put him back in the hospital again before he finally got his new lung. So what? All the greats were blessed with short memories. You had to forget that missed free throw and keep on playing. Don pushed that list of failures away and consoled himself by imagining a celebration of his own. His own party. He'd have Jackson and George from the coffee shop over for drinks in the backyard, but not Pete. Forget Pete, the interloper who'd moved to Lanier from California. Pete would not be invited. Don could grill some steaks. Joyce had fixed everything up out in the back yard while he was in the hospital, and at first, he'd hated it. Not the furniture itself but that she hadn't consulted him. She hadn't *consulted*. She'd just *done*.

But then he had to admit that the chairs were more comfortable. The twinkle lights she'd strung everywhere reminded him of the county fair when they had both been young and they'd had their first kiss under the Ferris wheel. Maybe that was what Joyce had been thinking of too.

The yard was okay and it would be a good place to sit with the boys and drink beer and eat food that wasn't good for them and celebrate Don's new lease on life. Jackson and George had never been to his house. He'd never seen either of them anywhere but the coffee shop, but that could change. So many things could change now.

Don took in a deep breath and his hand reached for the oxygen tank without even thinking. It was reflex, he'd lived with the tank so long. But now it was gone. It was time to move on. He didn't miss the tank. Not one bit.

"So it's all over." Jackson pulled out a chair, leaving one empty between him and Don. Jackson never came too close.

"What's all over?" Don looked around the room in confusion. That was his default condition lately. Confusion.

Jackson gestured at one side of his chest. "The Covid. Your lung. All healed up now. Happy ending."

"Right. Exactly." Don felt through the thin fabric of his shirt at the scar on his chest. It was so much smaller than he thought it should be.

"Cheers to that." Jackson lifted his beer and clicked it against Don's bourbon.

Don nodded. He glanced down at the glass but didn't take a drink.

"Treat this lung with care," Don's doctor had cautioned him. "Treat your body as precious. It is now."

Precious. Fragile.

"That's right," Don said. "A happy ending." He took a long drink of the bourbon, let it burn on the way down, a good burning. A healthy burning, not an oxygen-deprived one. He clapped Jackson on the back. "Cheers to that!" he shouted.

The people at the next table looked over. A few of them raised their glasses. Well, why not? Was it a party or wasn't it?

"I'm thinking someday soon maybe you and George could come over for steaks in the backyard," Don said. He put his hand on Jackson's forearm and squeezed. He'd never touched Jackson and now he had twice within a minute. It was a good sign. Anything was possible. "A celebration with just us guys."

Don could picture the three of them in the backyard, the embers of the grill still smoking and the fireflies coming up out of his perfectly mowed grass. And cigars. Maybe they'd have cigars too.

"Who's that?" Jackson asked. His voice was low, laced with wonder or fear. Don couldn't say for sure.

"Who?" Don surveyed the room. He didn't know half the people here, so he probably wouldn't know even if Jackson pointed them out.

"Who *are* they?" Jackson's voice was a whisper, the pupils of his eyes dark and wide.

"What are you talking about?" Don wished Jackson would get to the point so he could go back to contemplating backyard steaks. He scanned the crowd again. Was Julie here? Surely not. Joyce might have been different since he'd come out of the hospital, with her painting classes and her new friends, but she hadn't changed so much as to become the sort of woman who would invite his mistress to a party.

"You see them, don't you?" Jackson glanced at Don and nodded toward the front of the Blue Door.

The light grew dimmer and Don wondered if someone was playing with the switch somewhere. He looked in the direction Jackson had gestured and saw two women silhouetted against the brightness of the windows. They stood just inside the door, unmoving. That wasn't so strange. But as his eyes adjusted, he could understand Jackson's reaction. The women didn't fit. They weren't right. He couldn't say exactly what it was about them. Maybe the slow way they surveyed the room. Or how they leaned in close to each other. Their stillness, maybe? All Don knew for sure was that they shouldn't be there.

He glanced at Joyce, but she hadn't spotted them. She stood by one of the high tables, her body leaned close to someone Don didn't know. Maybe that painting teacher? Her face now was creased in an expression of deep concentration, as if she could not bear to miss a single word of what the guy was saying, so, no, she had not noticed the women. No one but Don and Jackson had noticed the women.

"I see them," Don said.

The women took a step forward into the room and a little of the strangeness around them resolved. They stuck out, but as they passed a group of people from the college, the volleyball coach turned to follow them and that was reassuring. They were real, at least.

"Party crashers, maybe," Jackson said. He tapped his beer against the table as if for reassurance.

"Or could be they're friends of Heather's," Don said. He looked at his daughter, who was reaching out to grab at Bethany as she darted by and missing, her face falling in that look of parental resignation and fatigue Don remembered so well. He looked back at the women undulating their way across the room. There was no way they were friends of Heather.

Were the two women sisters? He studied the long, white legs of the one in cutoff shorts. No, they were mother and daughter, but nothing like Joyce and Heather. The daughter linked her arm through her mother's, a gesture he had never once seen Joyce and Heather make. It was too spontaneous. Too easy. In their family, affection had its agreed-upon time and place.

Heads turned in the women's direction, a wave of motion rippling across the crowd as they made their way into the room. Sitting beside Don, Jackson went still.

There was a bar at the back of the long room that made up the Blue Door and that had to be where the women were headed. What else could have drawn them inside? They thought it was a bar. Or they knew it was a party and they were going to take advantage of the free booze. Party crashers, like Jackson said.

Joyce was between them and the bar. She would stop them. She was not a woman who would tolerate strangers at her party. That had not changed. Certainly not these strangers, who dripped with otherness and condescension. The daughter's boobs were practically falling out of her shirt and the mother wasn't much better. Who dressed like that on a Saturday afternoon in Lanier? No one.

The women drew even with the little cluster of people who stood around Joyce. A couple of the grandkids and a young woman. Was that the Emily that Joyce was always talking about?

Joyce's head turned toward the women with a motion so sharp it was athletic, like one of Don's best point guards surveying the court for the perfect pass. Joyce was her own sort of virtuoso, after all, queen of the quiet comment that proclaimed her will into the world. Don had never wanted a mousy woman for a wife. Joyce was Midwest steel. She would put those women in their place so gently they'd have no idea what had hit them.

Joyce took a step toward the women. She stopped. Her back was turned, so Don couldn't see the expression on her face. He couldn't hear what Joyce said, but he saw the straight lines of her back. The patch of white skin on her neck visible below her short hair. He had faith in Joyce and her steadiness. He watched the older woman's face, waiting for her smile to deflate as Joyce put her in her place.

Instead, the woman threw her head back and laughed. The daughter smiled, a small smile, her eyes moving from her mother's face to Joyce's and back. Joyce reached out a hand toward the woman's arm. As if they had practiced it ahead of time, Joyce turned and linked her arm with the woman's. All three of them zeroed in on Don, whose palms began to sweat. As one, they began to move toward him, a trio of women. Young. Older. Oldest.

Don drained the last of the bourbon in his glass. A drop escaped to dribble down his chin. He pushed himself up from the chair and then Don Blankman ran.

>>

Before the pandemic and the hospital and the lung transplant, Don and Joyce had talked about going to Ireland. Joyce's sister and brother-in-law had gone and they couldn't stop going on and on about it every time they came down to Lanier for lunch, which was entirely too often in Don's opinion.

"What do you think?" Don had asked Joyce one night as they lay in bed, the basketball game on but neither of them really watching. "Should we go to Ireland?"

"Who?" Joyce had pushed her readers up onto her nose. "Us?"

"Yes, us." Don had chuckled. "Why not us?"

They'd gotten as far as getting their passports renewed and then March had come and the world fell apart. Don hadn't forgotten though. Sometimes in the lowest moments of the past three years, he'd imagined him and Joyce in Ireland. They'd be standing on a cliff or sitting in a pub, listening to folk music. Ireland would be exotic in just the right amount. Different, but the same, and then *they* would have all the stories to tell.

They could do the trip now. There was nothing stopping them. Don thought about bringing it up sometimes, but he never did. He imagined that long flight across the ocean and his heart began to race. He was too fragile. It was too uncertain.

He didn't know why he thought about that trip now, as he ran down the alley behind the Blue Door, away from his wife and the women, his new lung miraculously keeping up, though his legs got tired quicker than they used to. Don didn't know what Ireland looked like, but surely not like the alleys of Lanier, which at the moment were foreign and strange. Like the time he'd ridden in the back of the golf cart instead of the front and the streets of Lanier in reverse had become unrecognizable.

As he ran, he saw strange graffiti, a black-and-white drawing of great, dark wings on the back of a fence. He saw kaleidoscopic murals he'd never known existed. He saw a garden of tomatoes and peppers, riotous with fruit, grown on top of the slanting roof of a back shed. He saw a stained-glass window and he saw garbage. Lots and lots of garbage.

When he came to the nearest cross street, he had no idea where he was. He'd lived in Lanier his whole life and now he was lost and terrified, glancing behind him, expecting to see the three women in pursuit. Or to see them step out of one of the doorways in front of him, having somehow teleported ahead. Their movements didn't follow the laws of physics.

He stopped to catch his breath, to feel the fill and empty of this lung that was not his own. This lung that would never be his own. He leaned back and stared up at the long section of white-blue August sky visible at the top of the building. Chimney swifts whirled by in a tight formation. He could almost hear their high-pitched chirping over the pounding in his ears.

From somewhere came a drift of music. Voices. Farther away, what sounded like a basketball being dribbled on pavement. He moved toward that sound and the comfort it implied. He turned down another alley, no more familiar than the last, but at the end of it, he found himself standing next to the coffee shop. The sound of a basketball dribbling was gone. Maybe he had never heard it at all.

The smell of coffee drifted out as someone opened the door to go inside. Joyce said she always knew where Don had been because of the smell of coffee on his clothes. He'd never asked if it was a smell she liked. Or hated. Or if she felt nothing at all about his smell.

Joyce smelled most often of outside and sweat when she'd been weeding in the garden. Or her fancy shampoo straight out of the bath. Lately, she smelled of a strange scent it had taken Don a long time to identify as oil paint and turpentine. When he caught that scent on Joyce, it felt like she was someone different. Not his wife. A stranger.

He stepped inside the coffee shop but didn't recognize the young woman behind the counter. The light was different this time of day. His regular table was empty. He got a cup of coffee and a donut and sat. He felt the lung begin to quiet. His heart began to slow. He was safe here. The women could not find him.

The women could not find him here and take him away. That was what they were there for. It didn't matter who had sent them. It didn't matter where they would go from there. They were a sign of the end and Don had run from it.

"What on earth, Don?"

He looked up to see Joyce, standing above him. The lung clenched for a moment, but she was alone. She smelled of red wine and a summer rain shower. Outside, uncertain drops fell onto the sidewalk.

"It got too stuffy," Don said. "I couldn't breathe in there."

"You didn't have to run away though," she said.

Don stared at his hands, wrapped around the coffee cup. He pushed them against the table to hide their shaking.

Joyce glanced around the mostly empty space of the coffee shop. "So this is the place, huh?"

Don didn't bother dignifying that with an answer. Joyce had been in the coffee shop before.

"Is this your table?" She gestured toward where he sat.

He nodded. No doubt, she knew that too. It wasn't like there were a lot of secrets in Lanier.

Joyce smoothed the fabric of her dress and lowered herself into the seat across from Don. She leaned an elbow on the table and it wobbled, which Don knew it would. That was not a thing he or Jackson or George cared about when they gathered here. Let the table wobble. The wobble felt, in fact, like an act of defiance. He dared Joyce to comment. She didn't.

He stared into the black depths of his coffee and waited for Joyce to tell him who the women were and where they'd gone. He waited for his wife to explain why she'd joined forces with the women. An explanation for why she had not defended him. For why she had not sent the women away with their tails between their legs.

But Joyce did not explain. She leaned one elbow on the wobbly table and stared out the window as the rain picked up.

"I'm not the same person now, you know," Don said. He touched a finger to the scar he could feel through his shirt.

"Neither am I." Joyce studied the tips of her fingers.

He waited for her to say more, but she didn't, so neither did he. He wondered who was in charge of the party if Joyce was here. He knew better than to think his leaving had had any effect one way or the other.

"Maybe we should move," Don said. It wasn't something he would've said had even occurred to him, but the words were famil-iar, as if they'd been in his head for a while. He just didn't know it.

"Move where?" Joyce said.

"Florida." Don shrugged. "Isn't that what you're supposed to do at our age? Isn't that what everyone is doing now? Going to live some-place new?"

No one Don knew had moved, but he'd seen a whole video about it on Facebook. The great post-pandemic migration. Mostly people leaving California and who could blame them?

"I don't want to live in Florida," Joyce said. "I'd miss the winter."

"That is true." Don tried to sound philosophical.

"Maybe a trip though," Joyce said.

"Ireland?" Don pictured that pub again. The simpler life of the people there. He imagined Ireland as some better version of an America he'd never actually experienced himself, but he was sure someone had. In that better version, everything was greener. Simpler. Clearer in some way Don couldn't put his finger on, like distances disappeared. People still trusted each other in that better America and accepted their lot in life instead of complaining all the time about how the world had wronged them. If that idea of America wasn't true, what was even the point of it all?

"Not Ireland," Joyce said. "Paris." Her lips curved into a tiny smile as she stared out the window, as if she could see the streets of Paris even now.

"Hmph," Don said.

The thought of going to Paris made Don's insides slick and hot. He burped and a little bit of the coffee came back up. The French hated Americans and the people didn't work for months during the summer. The whole damn country shut down.

"Who were those women?" he whispered. Even now, he was afraid to look over his shoulder toward the windows that lined the front of the coffee shop. He knew he would see the two women standing there, watching him and laughing.

"Oh, they just wandered in, looking for an adventure." Joyce wiped the crumbs from some former occupant onto the floor. "Didn't they look interesting?"

Don could not find his voice to answer. He could not tell Joyce why he had run. He could not tell her that in some twisted, bourbon-induced spell, he'd become convinced that the women were Death itself, come for him at last.

He'd thought, all those long months in the hospital and then waiting for the transplant, that he was ready. Let death come. Don Blankman wasn't afraid. But when he'd seen those women, he knew he was wrong. He was a coward and he had run.

He stared at Joyce's hand, laid against the table. He studied her crooked pinkie finger, where the arthritis was especially bad. She didn't let it stop her though. She didn't complain. Just sometimes when she thought no one was looking, she ran her fingers up and down the pinkie, as if that would smooth out the pain.

"Paris is for lovers," Don said.

Joyce laughed. "Paris is for artists." She closed her eyes. "They say the light is different there. Softer." She smiled again. "I want to be caught in a Paris rain."

Don pictured the two of them, huddled under an awning in a different version of Lanier's streets. He didn't have a clear picture of Paris in his head. But he liked the idea of having to huddle up close to Joyce, the two of them, safe and dry together.

"Paris, then," Don said.

Maybe they would go. Maybe they wouldn't. It felt like nothing to give Joyce the possibility. It felt like nothing to sit with it for a moment.

"We should get back," Joyce said. "They'll all be wondering where we are."

But neither of them moved. They sat at the table and watched the rain fall.

>>

Everyone knew when the nymphs left town. The riverboat calliope organ played as the boat began to drift away from the shore. The sound echoed through the valley. The songs were upbeat, but the tone was sad—the music of parting. The calliope played the melody of loss.

For the next week or so, the townsfolk told their stories. They compared notes over a beer in the Main Street Saloon. The women had gotten drunk at the bar. They'd stolen from the shops. They'd bought a house and were coming back. They'd crashed a party.

The river knew the truth, but it wasn't telling. People came and people went. The river spat them up onto the shore or carried them away. It was all the same. The river moved on.

Shampoo

Every Saturday for the next two months, Loretta swore she would not go see Dan Fortlow, the hot dog guy. She made long lists of all the things she needed to do over the weekend instead of seeing Dan Fortlow. She planned trips to the big pet store in Louisville where she could get Gus the special cat food the vet insisted would restore him to full cat health. She recorded hours and hours of late-night TV and PBS documentaries and the reality shows she hated, but which would take all day Saturday to catch up on. She spent hours shopping online for a new couch but could never bring herself to actually push the button that would bring the unfamiliar piece of furniture into her life.

None of it worked. All her complicated plans for avoiding the hot dog guy fell flat. Every Saturday, usually around twelve forty-five, right before the farmer's market closed, Loretta would stumble out of her front door like a drunk, blinking into the bright light or hunching her shoulders against the warm drizzle. The first Saturday when it rained, she prayed the market would be closed, but no, they were all still there. The hot dog guy too. What foolhardy persistence was this?

On sunny days, the line at the hog dog cart was long, even as the other vendors packed up behind him to leave. Other days, it was just Loretta, huddling under the hot dog guy's bright orange and yellow umbrella.

Sunshine or gloom, Dan Fortlow always acted happy to see her. He never took down his umbrella and told her he had somewhere else to be. He never looked around, desperation in his eyes, for someone to save him from Loretta's endless chatter.

Because her chatter *was* endless. Dan Fortlow had to be pretending to be happy to see Loretta, because she knew she was annoying as hell. She was annoying to herself. Of course she was annoying to the hot dog guy.

"How's your week been?" Dan Fortlow would ask. He never said, "What the hell are you doing here again? No one loves hot dogs this much," which was exactly what Loretta would have said in his place.

He did not ask Loretta for her name. She did not reveal that she knew his. The regulation Loretta had written to stop the hot dog guy in his tracks remained in limbo as the lawyers studied past precedents. If Dan Fortlow knew how precarious his livelihood was, he gave no sign.

They talked at first about hot dogs. Their history. Their status as authentic American food. Why Dan preferred the all-beef variety. If he believed there were rat tails mixed into the meat, which was what Tom had told Loretta in fourth grade. Yes, Loretta asked Dan Fortlow that and, still, he kept talking to her. What was the matter with this man?

She told him about her mom's illness and leaving grad school, though afterward, she couldn't reconstruct how that topic had come up.

"Do you think you're a bad mother if your child tells you she loves you and you don't respond?" she asked Dan Fortlow one Saturday when the first tomatoes appeared at the market.

"I make a policy not to judge," he said. "But gosh, that sure would hurt if you were that kid, wouldn't it?"

She thought for a while with all his "gosh" and "gollies" that he must be crazy religious. She hoped for it. Sure, Loretta went to church, but she wasn't a Jesus freak. She had no room for any more judgment in her life. She could stop all of this if Dan Fortlow were a Jesus freak.

"Oh, my parents were UU—Unitarian Universalists—but I don't much do that," he said when she asked.

So he wasn't a Jesus freak. Just a regular one.

They talked about the sex survey because it was still what everyone was talking about, even Dan Fortlow.

"I'm a little afraid to take it," Dan Fortlow admitted. "What if it tells me at the end that I'm some sort of sexual pervert, right?" He laughed. Was it a nervous laugh?

"Well, are you?" Loretta could not keep herself from asking.

Dan Fortlow turned a bright red and then changed the subject.

"What's going on with you and the hot dog guy?" Rachel asked. Rachel had stopped by Loretta's to pick up a box of old sketchbooks Loretta had found in a closet and offered free to the first taker. She had no idea where the sketchbooks had come from. They were all blank and high quality. Loretta stared at them for a long moment and imagined herself filling them with sketches and doodles. She would fill them with deep reflections on her life. Or meaningful poetry. But that wasn't who she was. It wasn't who she was ever going to be.

"Nothing's going on with me and the hot dog guy." Loretta handed the bag full of sketchbooks to Rachel and sat down on her front stoop. She pulled out a cigarette and gestured at the spot beside her.

Rachel sat down. "I've seen you talking to him every Saturday I've been at the farmer's market."

"He makes a good hot dog." Loretta shrugged. "What are you going to do with all these notebooks?"

Rachel went on about the writing thing she'd been to in Florida and something called morning pages, but Loretta was only half listening. She was thinking about the contents of the rest of the closet. She couldn't give everything away. She'd have to toss most of it. Maybe Dan Fortlow would want some things though. She imagined holding each item up in front of Dan Fortlow, one by one. Would he want all the empty shoeboxes Grandma had saved just in case but never filled? The countless measuring cups someone had acquired? The Christmas-y glasses that had never once held a drop of eggnog? Her junk could be a Rorschach test for the hot dog guy. What would he want and what would he reject?

"Do you ever have trouble throwing things away?" she asked Dan Fortlow the next Saturday. There was some kids' activity going on at the farmer's market, so Loretta had to shout over the noise of screaming children.

"No, ma'am." Dan Fortlow gave the mustard bottle a little squeeze for emphasis, which he often did. Just enough to make a tiny puff of air, but not enough to expel any actual mustard. It was a skill Loretta admired greatly. "Every six months, I have a purging. I make a big pile of stuff and take it to Goodwill. The rest of it, I burn." He tilted his head. "Assuming it's not toxic, of course. Don't want to release any bad fumes into the air as part of your purging."

"But there's nothing you keep?" She watched a mother chase down a kid and grab him hard by his arm. She winced. "Like things that have sentimental value? That belonged to your family?"

Loretta genuinely wanted to know the answer to this question. She was also fishing for information about Dan Fortlow's family, which he had never mentioned. He wore no wedding ring. He never mentioned a partner. She knew he had a dog he worried about leaving alone for so long during the market. She knew he'd moved to

Lanier five years ago. She didn't know why. The endless opportunities for hot dog sales?

She felt too guilty to ask Dan Fortlow for details about his life. She was the one, after all, who was trying to ruin it.

"Well, does keeping an object really help me remember something I wouldn't otherwise? Does it bring me any closer to that person?" He tapped his fingers against the metal lid of the cart, considering. "I don't think so. Besides, everything is fleeting. Stuff. People. Memories."

"That's depressing," Loretta said.

"No. It's freeing." Dan Fortlow nodded and pointed a finger at Loretta. "Try it. Throw something away. See how much lighter you feel. Like you could float away." He wiggled his fingers as he lifted his hands, like a butterfly taking flight.

Loretta frowned and watched the kid being led away by his mom, sobbing and screaming, "I hate you!" over and over again.

She had never felt light enough to float away and she couldn't imagine it happening now.

>>

Loretta had told Dan Fortlow where she lived. It was what you did in Lanier—told people where you lived. You tried to describe in exact detail where your house was until their face lit up with recognition. Even if they were faking, it didn't matter. You had to keep going until that moment came.

Of course, with Dan Fortlow, she couldn't say that she lived across the street from her kindergarten teacher and anyway, Mrs. Hendrickson had died. Mrs. Hendrickson, who would never, ever be Vicki to Loretta, though when Loretta had moved back to Lanier, she'd insisted over and over that Loretta call her that. Mrs. Hendrickson and her husband had both died from Covid, though they had been pretty frail at that point. It still felt like a blow. Like the ending of something important in Loretta's life.

Dan Fortlow didn't know any of that intimate geography, so Loretta had to explain and explain, from one cross street to the next until he finally arrived at an image of her house.

"The house with the chandeliers on the porch?" Dan Fortlow asked.

"No, not that one." Loretta hated that house and their chandeliers. "Other side of the street. Green with a black iron fence."

"Next to that dog that waits until you're right in front of the yard to start barking and scares the crap out of you?" he asked.

"Yeah, that one."

He hadn't offered up his own house, but then, he didn't need to. Loretta already knew where he lived.

She'd told him where her house was and she'd probably even said, "Stop by sometime," because that was also what you said. It was what Loretta's mom had always said, though no one had ever taken her up on the offer except her best friend, Bev, who came by to beg her mom to join a book club or the gardener's club or whatever club Bev was into at the moment. Her mom had always refused. "I don't like people," she would grumble.

So Loretta didn't expect Dan Fortlow to actually show up at her house. When he knocked on the door, she assumed it was Tom.

"I'm not going for another walk," she said as she opened the door. But instead of Tom, it was Dan Fortlow, in a collared shirt and khaki pants. Dressed up. He was dressed up. What was happening?

"We don't have to go for a walk," Dan Fortlow said. He shuffled his feet, his hand running over the surface of the iron railing on Loretta's stoop. "Though we could if you wanted to."

Loretta stared at Dan Fortlow. She looked behind him, as if some other person would appear to make his presence on her doorstep comprehensible.

"This is weird, isn't it?" He took a step away, down one of the steps that led back onto the sidewalk. "I'm going."

"No." Loretta reached out a hand, but not far enough to touch him. He stopped, one foot on the top step and one on the stoop. "I mean, yeah, it's weird. But weird is okay."

"I'm Dan, by the way," the hot dog guy said.

"Yeah, I know," Loretta started to answer, but stopped herself. She was not supposed to know his name.

"Loretta." She pointed to a spot between her boobs, like a total idiot. Like her name was tattooed there. It was not.

>>

Loretta couldn't remember the last time a man besides Tom had been inside her house. Maybe Mr. Kelley, who'd fixed the toilet? But neither Tom nor Mr. Kelley had taken up space the way Dan Fortlow did. He loomed. He was tall. Why hadn't she noticed that? The hot dog cart shrank him somehow. Her living room turned him into a giant. He wouldn't even fit on her couch lying down. Why was she thinking about him lying down on her couch?

"I like the way these downtown houses are . . ." He made a gesture with his arms, like an air traffic controller directing a plane on the runway. "You know. *Whoosh.*"

"*Whoosh*?" What was he talking about? She couldn't concentrate as she searched the room for a discarded bra or underwear or a tampon or some other humiliating evidence of the abject sadness of her life.

"Like, you can stand at the front door and see all the way to the back," Dan Fortlow said. "*Whoosh.*"

"Right." Well, he would be able to see all the way to the back of her house if it wasn't full of so much junk. "Do you want something to drink?" Loretta asked.

It was seven thirty. Too early for his visit to verge into late-night creepy, but late enough not to interfere with dinner, if Loretta ate such a thing. Most nights a bag of microwave popcorn passed for dinner, with an apple for dessert so she at least got some nutrients into her body.

"Sure." Dan Fortlow shoved his hands into his pockets. There was a long pause. "What have you got?"

Right, Loretta was supposed to offer him specific things. That was what a host did. She closed her eyes and pictured the contents of her kitchen. Bourbon. She had bourbon. Some apple juice. Could she make a drink out of that?

"Or, you know, I don't really need anything." He scuffed his feet against her rug.

Her stained, threadbare rug that had been peed and puked on by countless generations of cats, though, at the moment, Gus was nowhere in sight. No doubt he was hiding, as freaked out by the sight of a man in the house as Loretta was.

She squinted up at the giant that was Dan Fortlow. She didn't need this. She didn't need his awkward politeness. She hadn't asked for it.

"What are you doing here?" She felt the anger stiffen her spine, pulling her upright. Taking back a little of her space. It *was* her space. "Who does this? Just knocks on a stranger's door?" There was something familiar in the tone of her voice. What was it?

Dan Fortlow's shoulders sagged. He bowed his head. "I know." His voice was barely a whisper. "I'll go."

But he didn't move and neither did Loretta. They both stood there, Dan Fortlow staring at his feet. Loretta studying the top of his head, which was not balding like almost every other man she knew at this point in her life.

She was about to tell him to get out when she remembered what was familiar about her voice. She sounded like her mom. Each word tuned to the perfect mix of anger and disdain. How could she ever have forgotten? She'd heard that voice so often. She felt sometimes that voice lived inside her always, like a stone at the bottom of her throat. Like a whisper behind her ear. "No one loves you, Loretta," that voice whispered. "How could they?"

"Oh, for fuck's sake," Loretta said. "Just sit down."

She was surprised when Dan Fortlow did.

>>

They talked about the lateness of spring that year. The little pink dogwood in front of Loretta's house that she was afraid would be blasted in a morning frost. Dan Fortlow had a dwarf peach tree in his backyard he was equally concerned about. He had a small green-house, one he'd built himself, following an instructional video on YouTube. He was trying to grow cucumbers and dill year-round for his pickle relish. He was having limited success.

Dan Fortlow talked about the farmer's market and the other ven-dors. The petty fights that erupted every week. The way the farmer's market manager seemed to delight in calling the police when one of the people on the street they closed off for the market hadn't moved their car. The way the police didn't seem to mind, which made Dan wonder what it might be like, to be a police officer in Lanier.

Loretta talked about her decluttering project. About the take-away dumpsters she had priced to make the whole process easier. But living downtown, it wasn't like she had a driveway to park the dumpster in. It would have to go out on the street and then the neighbors would complain. Or worse, they'd talk about her to each other, behind her back. She would know they were upset, but like true Midwesterners, they'd never say anything to her face. She had played it all out in her head and it didn't end well.

"But maybe you could just tell them ahead of time. Explain and ask if it was okay, and then they wouldn't get mad." Dan Fortlow was an eternal optimist.

"Well, it costs a lot too," Loretta said.

They lapsed into an awkward silence then. She still didn't know what he was doing here. Outside, it was getting dark. Normally, she'd be in bed, reading a book by now. A horror novel or true crime. The more gruesome the better. Because of her reading, she was fully cognizant of the horrifying ways Dan Fortlow could kill her and dispose of her body. No one would know. No one would suspect him, besides maybe Rachel. Still, she went on sitting on the couch. Getting drowsy, even. Maybe he'd sprayed some sort of sedative into the air.

"I have a favor to ask, Loretta," Dan Fortlow said.

Loretta sat up. Here it was. This was it. He would invite her for a ride in his van. Or a nighttime walk along the Heritage Trail, which was secluded and too far from any house for anyone to hear her screams.

But, also, this was the first time Dan Fortlow had ever said her name and there was something about the way he emphasized the 't' sound (Lo-rettt-uh) that made it sound interesting. Exotic, even.

"Okay," she whispered.

He laced his hands together in his lap. To keep them from reaching out and strangling her? He cleared his throat.

"Could I wash your hair, Loretta?" He glanced very quickly up from his hands still folded in his lap at Loretta and then back down. His face was the bright red it had been when she asked him about the sex survey all those weeks ago.

"Wash my hair," Loretta repeated. In some diversity training at the health department, they'd taught them about looping. Saying back to the other person what you heard. It was supposed to be a great way to avoid intractable conflict. "You want to wash my hair."

"It's not a sex thing." Dan Fortlow's two hands in his lap gripped each other tightly. His face contorted into a look of pain. "I just like washing women's hair."

"Okay." Loretta sat back on the sofa. She wanted a cigarette, but she was trying not to smoke in the house. "Why aren't you like a hair-dresser then?"

Didn't that make sense? If Dan Fortlow liked washing women's hair so much that he was willing to ask a stranger, hairdresser was sort of like his career of destiny, wasn't it?

"Yeah, I tried that." He looked up at Loretta, willing her to under-stand. His hands stayed clasped in his lap. "It didn't work. It was . . . a job. You know? It didn't feel right."

Loretta reached up and wrapped a strand of hair around her finger. It could use a wash, truth be told. She sat up and studied Dan Fortlow, a picture of discomfort and shame. She was intrigued, like Dan Fortlow's hair thing was part of the diary of a nineteenth-century midwife she'd been obsessed with long ago, her handwriting spidery and sprawled and difficult to decipher. But when she had figured it out, Loretta had been the only person in the world who knew what that midwife had said. She was the only one who knew exactly what she used the comfrey for. Loretta hadn't thought for a long time about how satisfying that feeling had been.

"So, what makes it feel right?" she asked.

Do you wash your girlfriend's hair, she wanted to add. Your mother's? How does this work exactly? Who am I to you? Where do I fit in?

Dan Fortlow took in a long breath and then let it out. "I guess I'm still figuring that out." He stared up at the ceiling. "There was this older lady. My neighbor. She had beautiful, long, white hair. She had shoulder replacement surgery and she couldn't wash her hair, so I offered. To wash it in the sink, you know. She didn't have any family who lived close." His lips turned up in the smallest suggestion of a smile. "She thought it was weird at first, I could tell. But then she let me. And when her shoulder healed, we just . . . didn't stop."

"So what happened?" Loretta searched her memory for stories about the death or disappearance of an older woman on the Hilltop, in her old neighborhood. She could look back at the obituaries later, if Dan Fortlow didn't murder her.

"She moved away." Dan Fortlow shrugged.

"And now you're here," she said.

"And now I'm here." Dan Fortlow returned his attention to his hands.

Loretta listened to the sound of voices passing on the side-walk outside. She could call out to them. Make a break for the door. Scream for help. Her brain idly turned over these possibilities, but she didn't feel afraid. She didn't feel in danger. She wasn't sure what she felt. She was enjoying the silence, the opportunity to dig around inside her head to figure out exactly what was going on up there.

"You have beautiful hair," Dan Fortlow whispered into the silence. "It was the first thing I noticed about you."

"Would this mean we were dating or something?" Loretta said. "Because I don't want to be dating a hot dog guy."

She expected Dan Fortlow to cringe. Or puff up with anger. She expected him to get up and leave. He didn't do any of those things.

"No, we wouldn't be dating," he said. "I'd just be . . . you know. Washing your hair."

Loretta studied Dan Fortlow's face. It was different in the faded light of her living room than in the brightness of the farmer's market. Softer. Flatter. She didn't have an artistic bone in her body, but she wished she did. She wished she could capture Dan Fortlow right now, sitting on her couch, begging her to let him wash her hair.

How desperate must his need be, to risk this? To reveal his tenderest part to her in this way? How brave it was. Loretta would never have that sort of courage. She'd perish from the wanting before she'd ever lay herself bare like this. That was the problem though, wasn't it?

"Why me?" she whispered. She gestured at what she thought of as her mousy, uninteresting head of hair. "Because of this?"

"Your hair is beautiful," Dan Fortlow assured her.

Loretta rolled her eyes.

"But also . . . ," Dan Fortlow said. "I don't know. I thought you might understand."

Loretta laughed, a harsh cackle in the quiet of the room. "I don't understand."

"Okay."

"That's it?" she asked.

Dan Fortlow swallowed. He straightened his shoulders. He looked into Loretta's eyes. "You're lonely too." His eyes were shining, like he might be about to cry, which was not what Loretta needed. "I could see that you're hurt. You hurt."

So many words waited at the end of Loretta's tongue. All of them familiar. All of them cruel. It would take so little effort to cut Dan Fortlow down to his knees. She'd learned from a master.

Loretta's mom wouldn't hesitate to do it. Then, her mom wouldn't have let him in the house in the first place. Then, Dan Fortlow never would have asked her mom to wash her hair. Loretta wasn't her mom. Loretta was different.

She reached up and pulled the elastic band holding her hair in its tight ponytail out. Letting her hair down felt like letting out a breath. She brushed it behind her shoulders.

"Well." She raised her eyebrows at Dan Fortlow and the expectant look on his face. "Did you bring your own shampoo or what?"

The Reading

Rachel could not do this. No way. It was impossible, so what had she been thinking? What insane impulse had landed her here, sitting in the crowded coffee shop, waiting her turn to stand up and read her story to a room full of strangers and friends?

"This is great, but it'd be even better with bourbon," Nancy said. She sat at the next table with her new boyfriend, Dr. Harvey, and her daughter Liz.

"Right," Rachel said. She tried to smile or laugh but it came out more like a snort.

"You didn't smuggle in some booze, did you?" Nancy asked.

"Drinks at our place after." Charlie nodded at Nancy and gave Rachel a wink. "I'll make you a lovely cocktail, Nancy."

Right, Rachel thought. *Cocktails, not stories*. That's what Rachel was good at. She was a bartender, not a writer, and probably not even particularly good at that. She was a middle-aged woman who'd spent her whole life flitting from one job to another. Fickle, her narcissist ex-boyfriend had called her. His favorite activity had been telling her who she was, and twenty years later she was still sifting through his various proclamations. Rachel was fickle, he'd said, unable to settle on one thing or another for very long. She'd gone through a period after college when she'd been obsessed with professional wrestling. She wasn't embarrassed about it. Professional wrestling was fascinating. She'd followed all the storylines. The characters.

She knew the difference between a face and a heel. She read wrestler biographies and post-modern analyses. She paid for the big events and planned her life around them.

Then one day, she stopped. She hadn't watched wrestling in thirty years. She didn't miss it. Didn't think about it. Did that mean there was something wrong with her? A deep deficiency that had never gone away? Writers were serious people. Writers were committed people and Rachel was not.

This writing thing would end up the same way. She'd do it for a while, then quit. That was the truth. She should stand up and make an announcement right now. "I'm fickle! I'm a quitter! Beware!" She should apologize to all her friends for taking up their Thursday evening to be here in the first place.

"Are you nervous?" Sam leaned over and asked.

"Oh, maybe a little," Rachel said.

Her stepdaughter Sam had come home to get some winter clothes and not just to hear Rachel read a story at the coffee shop, because Rachel would never ask Sam to do that. It was well beyond the bounds of appropriate parental behavior. She'd had no intention of even mentioning the reading to Sam, but then Liz had brought it up when Sam came to see Rachel at the bar, and so now here Sam was, texting a running commentary on the event to her girlfriend, Ava, back in Bloomington.

"It's just like tending bar, right?" Sam said.

"Is it?" Rachel stretched her mouth into something that might pass for a smile and straightened the stack of pages that sat on the table in front of her.

If this was like tending bar, Rachel didn't see it. Being a bartender was a dance. The quick pirouette from tap to customer. The rhythmic gyration of the cocktail shaker. The back-and-forth of conversation with drunk people. It wasn't scripted. It wasn't stiff and formal, like this. It was improvisation and she could always walk away. There was always something calling to her, even if it was nothing more than a chat in the back hallway with Bryan, her boss, or the kitchen guys.

She loved tending bar, but each shift, she felt the end coming. She was forty-seven. She couldn't go on forever. Her body wouldn't allow it. Writing was the balance she hadn't known she needed. It was like traveling to the quiet core of herself. It was the opposite of bartending, an excuse to be alone, with no needs to meet but the page's and her own.

How did that quiet connect to the noise and chaos in the coffee shop right now? The nervous energy of people about to cut themselves open and bare their tenderest parts to the world?

"Oh, do you remember that survey you told me about a while ago?" Sam was talking to Charlie.

"Yeah, I remember," Charlie said. "The sex survey."

At the front of the coffee shop, in the little space they'd carved out for a stage, the poet who taught at the high school stood up and looked around expectantly. She didn't have a microphone. She tried clearing her throat a couple of times, but no one else was paying her much attention.

"I found something out about it," Sam said. "At a party in Bloomington."

"What?" The frantic tone of Rachel's voice cut through the low hum of the coffee shop conversation. Everyone turned to her and the poet took advantage of the silence to speak.

"Welcome to open mic night on Main Street," the poet said. The attention of the crowd shifted toward her, polite and expectant.

"What did you hear?" Rachel whispered at Sam, but in the new quiet, her voice was too loud. How could Sam bring this up *now*, right before Rachel was about to reveal what a complete idiot she was in front of everyone she knew?

Sam shook her head in an admonishing way and nodded toward the poet.

What? She couldn't tell Rachel *now*? It wasn't like they were at church or something. Who had raised this slavishly obedient child? Rachel had not taught her this.

Rachel looked at Charlie, but his attention was on the poet, who was reading some kind of welcome speech. Or maybe it was a poem? Rachel wasn't paying attention.

After all these months, Rachel assumed Sam had never gotten the survey. She thought it had all passed Sam by. Rachel certainly hadn't said anything to Sam about it. But Charlie had? Why? How had it even come up?

Rachel had been in a strange panic when the survey had arrived in Lanier inboxes that January. She'd felt a slow-burning fear that she told herself was about Sam and the survey but, in the end, didn't have anything to do with that. That fear had driven her to Florida and that moment on the beach, all the signs of a post-pandemic, middle-age collapse. The survey had become associated in her mind with that period of free fall.

She was better now—calmer—but something about the survey reappearing at this moment pulled her back into that old terror.

In her darkest moments, Rachel had felt certain the survey was a sign. The survey was the big finger of the universe pointing at Lanier and Rachel and Charlie and Sam—singling them out for some sin they'd all committed or for how easy Rachel's life had been. For how happy she was with Charlie. For how much she loved living in Lanier, which she knew most people would never understand. She loved living in a small town in rural Indiana? What was the matter with her?

Rachel remembered the story the *New York Times* had done about Lanier five years ago, a rambling essay that had tried to string together a series of suicides and an opioid epidemic into a narrative about rural desolation. The town that reporter had described was unrecognizable to Rachel. She remembered how the Louisville TV station had gotten the name of the tiny, crossroads town outside of Madison wrong when it got hit by a tornado. Over and over again in her head, she saw the sneer on the faces of the people at the writer's conference when she'd told them she was from a small town in Indiana. The way one of the women had kept introducing her as from Idaho. They both started with I, so what was the difference?

The people behind the survey had not picked Lanier for all the reasons that made Rachel love the town. They picked it because it was twisted. They picked it as an example of everything that was wrong with the world. Nothing good happened when people turned their gaze to Lanier. The survey would be no exception.

Rachel picked up her phone and started to text Sam. Surely Sam could not resist answering a text.

"First up tonight is Rachel Barr," the poet announced.

The tables around Rachel erupted with shouting and clapping. Charlie banged on the table. Nancy put her two fingers against her lips and let out a whistle that made her new boyfriend cringe. "Get it, Rachel!" Liz yelled.

"No, no, no," Rachel whispered.

"Honey, you're up," Charlie said. He pointed toward the poet and the front of the room. "You'll knock 'em dead."

"No, no, no," Rachel said again. She pushed herself up out of her chair so quickly it would have fallen over if Sam hadn't caught it. She marched up to the poet, a mousy-looking woman in a long flowing skirt and a shirt with many small, embroidered flowers that Rachel had the feeling she had sewn herself—and then perhaps had written a poem about the process.

"Rachel appears to be a crowd favorite," the poet said. She smiled, but Rachel could tell she wasn't really happy about all the clapping and the noise.

"I can't go right now," Rachel leaned down and whispered at the poet-woman. "I can't go first."

"Oh." The poet-woman looked down at the list in her hands, written in a careful calligraphy, the name of each reader in a different color and illustrations running through the margins like some strange medieval manuscript. "But I assigned the order randomly. It's the fairest way to do it."

"Sure, that's great. Very smart." Rachel turned her back to the crowd, but she could still feel their eyes on her. "Just put me in another random spot."

"Yeah, Rachel!" Liz yelled again from her table.

Rachel couldn't read right now. She needed more time. Time to regroup after the survey had suddenly resurfaced in her life, threatening to tip her back into chaos. Time to find out what the hell Sam had meant. She couldn't stand up there reading with the survey taking up so much space in her brain. It was like a dark spot just out of the corner of Rachel's eye. She couldn't concentrate as long as it was there.

The poet-woman stared at her list. "How would I do that though? I need a random-number generator to figure out which spot you'd go in. Or maybe some dice. I don't have those. And to be fair, I'd have to rearrange the whole list, not just your spot."

"Put me at the end then," Rachel said. "No one wants to go last, right?"

Behind her, she could sense the crowd getting restless. It was a bartender superpower, the ability to read a crowd simply from the tone of their murmurings.

"The crowd thins out at the end, yes," the poet-woman said. "And there's a chance we'll run out of time. We have to stop right at eight. The coffee-shop workers have to have time to close up, you know."

The poet-woman said this with such virtuousness, Rachel wanted to laugh out loud. *Yes,* she wanted to say, *I know all about having to close up.*

"That's fine," Rachel said. "Absolutely fine. If we run out of time, we run out of time. No big deal. There's always next month, right?"

Her crowd would probably be bummed if they didn't get to hear Rachel read, but it wouldn't stop them from heading back to their house for drinks, a raucous group moving through the streets of Lanier. Her friends were easy to please. It wasn't the end of the world, even if the poet-woman acted like it was.

"Fine." The poet-woman pulled a pen out from behind her ear and very slowly crossed Rachel's name off its spot on the list.

"Thank you, thank you." Rachel resisted the urge to embrace the small woman in her gratitude.

The poet-woman didn't respond. She didn't look at Rachel. She stayed pointedly focused on her list.

"Right," Rachel mumbled.

She made her way back to the table, saved for the moment at least.

"So, first up," the poet-woman said, "George Nordan."

One of the old guys who hung out in the coffee shop in the morning pushed himself up out of his chair and worked his way toward the front of the room. In her haste to sit back down, Rachel almost bumped into Don Blankman, who was looking very displeased, but then, what was he doing at a reading anyway? It was hardly his scene.

Rachel tucked herself back into her chair. She was sweaty. Was she having a hot flash on top of everything else or was it just panic sweat?

"What happened there?" Charlie whispered.

Rachel shrugged. "I'm not the opening act. I'm the headliner."

Charlie raised an eyebrow and then turned his attention to George.

"This poem is about my first dog," George was saying. "Her name was Sandy. She was a golden retriever. She was the love of my life."

"Good grief," Don Blankman said. Someone shushed him.

Across the table, Sam had her phone in her lap and she was discreet, but she was clearly texting Ava. Rachel pulled out her own phone.

"What did you hear about the survey?" she texted. She watched Sam and saw the moment she got the text, the frown and then the little shake of her head.

"Someone said it was like a sexual Middletown," Sam texted. "Do you know what that is?"

"Yes," Rachel texted.

She glanced at Charlie, who was scowling at both of them. She tried to tune in to George's dog poem. He was describing the sweet smell of dog breath. Everyone paid good Midwestern attention as George marched through a series of dog-breath similes. Everyone except for Don Blankman, who obviously and repeatedly rolled his eyes. "Her breath was like chicken noodle soup on a sick day in bed. It was like the sweat in the high school locker room after winning the championship." George's similes went on and on.

Rachel knew about Middletown. Middletown was Muncie, Indiana. Not Lanier. A sociological study of a "typical" American town. The very idea was ridiculous now, that one town could ever possibly represent the whole of a country. It had been an attempt to erase everything unique about Muncie. To make it stand in for everyone. But no town could do that. Each town was its own thing.

A sexual Middletown. And someone had thought Lanier would be a good place for that? It was ridiculous. She wanted to laugh. She wanted to cry. She couldn't be sure which. Lately she felt so many things all at the same time, she didn't have the ability to sort them out.

"What else did you hear?" she texted Sam.

"Just that," Sam texted. "It was at a party." She looked up at Rachel and shrugged.

At the front of the coffee shop, George was using a single finger to wipe a couple of tears away. "Thank you for listening," he said and then shuffled back to his table.

"Christ," Don Blankman murmured.

"He really loved that dog," Charlie said.

"No kidding." Sam leaned toward Rachel. "Are you next?"

"No," Rachel said. "You don't know anything else about the survey?"

"No." Sam picked up her phone again. "That's it."

Rachel could hear the beginning of annoyance in Sam's voice.

The poet-woman announced the next reader. The door to the coffee shop opened and Loretta burst in. She pulled an empty chair over to their table and collapsed into it. She blew out a gust of air.

"What did I miss?" Loretta asked.

"Dog breath," Charlie said.

"Got it," Loretta said.

Rachel barely heard the rest of the readers. Someone recited a Walt Whitman poem with a surprising amount of enthusiasm. A young guy went on so long that the poet-woman had to stand next to

him for a full minute, clearing her throat over and over again, before
Don Blankman yelled, "Your time's up already, buddy!"

Why had the sex researchers picked Lanier? Had one of them
been here? Had they been living among them the whole time?
Rachel thought of the young guy who'd started showing up at the
Saloon over the summer, sitting at the bar with his copy of *Walden*,
which he never read. For a moment, she'd thought he might be
connected to the survey somehow, but it turned out he was just Joe
Amato's grandson.

Rachel understood how surveys worked. The moments she saw—
tiny flashes of joy and kindness and sacrifice—none of those would
show up in the answers. None of the surveys could explain why she
teared up at the Regatta parade every single year. She wasn't patriotic.
She hated the sirens of the police cars and worried that this would
be the year a kid would get run over by the little men in the Shriner
cars as they scurried into the street for candy. She couldn't explain
to anyone else why the parade made her cry. Something about the
way people came together, even if the mayor tried and failed every
year to keep the Rainbow River Club with all their bright flags and
wigs out of the parade. That all disappeared as half the town marched
down the street. There was something eternally hopeful about a
small-town parade. The survey would never capture that.

"Our final reader of the night is Rachel Barr," the poet-woman said.

The sound of her name jarred Rachel out of her reverie. She
looked down at the pages in front of her. There was no escaping this
time.

"You've got this," Charlie said. He squeezed her hand and then
let go.

Rachel stood and walked to the front of the coffee shop. She paid
careful attention to each step she took. Her crowd was cheering her

on again, if a little less enthusiastically than they had the first time around. It was late. The baristas looked impatient. Don Blankman might have fallen asleep, though George was still bright-eyed and awake. He nodded at Rachel as she took up her spot.

"Thanks," Rachel said. She stared at the passage she'd highlighted to read. It included what she thought was an especially perfect description of the way the sunlight sparkled on the river some days. Like diamonds, yes, but more than that. In the passage, she had tried to capture the way that light on the water was mirrored inside her heart or the soft matter of her brain or somewhere in the empty spaces of her stomach. She couldn't exactly locate the feeling, she just knew that seeing the sunlight on the river was a full-body experience and she wanted everyone else to feel it with her. She wanted everyone else to understand this revelation she'd come to—everything was a full-body experience because that was all humans were. Soft creatures with bodies they would never fully understand. How could they? Such a strange collection of cells and molecules and atoms and dark matter, which no one even knew what that was. How could anyone possibly hope to understand themself in the face of such mystery? Writing had given her that truth and she wanted to share it.

"Thanks," Rachel said again. It was so quiet in the coffee shop. Quiter than it ever got in the Saloon except when it was just her and Jackson in the long afternoon before her shift ended. She dared a glance up at the faces around her. Nancy caught her eye and gave her a thumbs up. Sam was looking at her phone again, which was a relief. Don Blankman was at least not rolling his eyes. He was too busy staring daggers at George beside him.

Rachel flipped through the pages to a different scene, the one she'd written back in Florida, back in those furious, lonely days when she had felt like something vast and incomprehensible was being channeled through her. It had burned out the tips of her fingers onto the page.

"This might be familiar to some of you," Rachel said. She cleared her throat, not because she needed to but because that seemed to be what people did before they began reading. She thought of whether there was something else she should say and then decided against it. Best to jump right in.

"In every restaurant or bar, there was a certain hour of the day or the week when the customers thinned out or disappeared altogether and everyone was so exhausted or giddy or bored that they lost their minds. At the Main Street Saloon, this usually happened on Wednesday at three thirty, and this was when Seth would begin to dance."

She had forgotten to change the name of the Saloon. She hadn't been certain if she should. She hadn't really even been sure if what she'd written was an essay or a story or something else. She had changed Joshua's name, though that wouldn't fool anyone. She knew Liz and Nancy and Bryan would all be smiling now. They'd seen Joshua dance.

"Like all good bars, the Saloon belonged to the regulars, but in the quiet moments, ownership reverted to the people who worked there, like soldiers in their barracks after the battle, it had that sort of spirit. They'd been through it and survived and now anything was possible. Anyway, if you'd ever worked in a good restaurant or bar, you knew the feeling." Rachel cringed. She could have been more specific there. It was a cheap sentence. Too easy. Too imprecise.

"At three thirty on Wednesdays, everyone was waiting and also pretending not to wait. The rules were that you couldn't ask Seth to dance. The rules were that you couldn't talk about Seth dancing. You just had to wait and see if it would happen. Seth would dance if the right song came on or a commercial on the TV or the replay of some football or baseball game. There was really no predicting what would set Seth off. Sometimes Shawnee could get him going by singing one of his favorite tunes as she married the ketchup bottles. Or Bryan's humming would do it. It was part of what made Seth's dancing so special. No one could control it. Seth would either dance or he wouldn't and there wasn't much any of them could do about it."

God, what a stupid passage she'd picked. She should've picked something more suspenseful, only, had she written anything with suspense? That was something she'd have to work on—creating suspense. No, she wouldn't have to work on that because, after this, she was done. She was giving up on this ridiculous writing thing. In fact, maybe she could stop right now. End with that last sentence and walk away. She had failed, after all, failed in whatever she was trying to do.

For a moment, she felt like she was back in that hotel room in Florida at the writer's conference, all by herself and being consumed by the emptiness that was at the bottom of everything. Nothing made sense. There was no reason the survey people had picked Lanier. Even if she learned what the reason was, it would be incomprehensible. There was no order. No reason. The emptiness was always there, waiting. It would always return, given the passage of time.

"I'm sorry," Rachel whispered. The words on the page blurred. She couldn't look up and see the faces of everyone as they watched and waited.

"You have to believe you are the only person on the planet who can tell this story," the famous author at the writer's conference had said. "You have to know that deep in the fiber of your being."

Why me though? Rachel wanted to know. And who cares? Who cares in the end about the story you have to tell?

Rachel risked a glance up from her page. Charlie was smiling, unworried. Sam had tilted back her cup, trying to get the last dregs of her caramel macchiato. Loretta looked bored, but Loretta always looked bored.

The poet-woman sat at a table all by herself. As Rachel looked at her, the poet-woman held up a small sign. Rachel had to squint to make it out. She should have worn her glasses.

"Just read the next word," the poet-woman's sign said. She didn't smile encouragingly at Rachel. She just held the sign, the same serious expression on her face.

Had she done this for everyone who read or just Rachel? Did it matter?

Just read the next word.

"Seth wasn't a good dancer," Rachel read. It was a good, solid sentence. Not too fancy. She took in a deep breath and went on. "He was fully aware of his lack of dancing skills. Seth was in every other way a joyless person." She heard the percussive snort that was Charlie's laughter. She didn't care if it was real or manufactured. She kept on reading. "But when he danced, he was transformed and maybe it was this that made them all crave his performances, the strange juxtaposition."

Rachel was glad Joshua wasn't actually there, though word would get back to him, wouldn't it, that she'd called him a joyless person. Only it wasn't quite Joshua she was describing. The person she had written about was something more and something less.

"That Wednesday it was raining and someone had left their umbrella by the door," Rachel read. "Seth picked up the discarded umbrella and before any of the more superstitious of the staff could stop him, he opened it up. When he danced, he moved like an old lady, his back hunched and his tiny steps tentative. His movements were so contained and also so exuberant. It didn't make sense. It was a small wonder, right there in the dreary light of the Saloon on a Wednesday afternoon."

The room was very quiet and Rachel wasn't sure if that was good or bad.

"Seth lifted the umbrella up and then down, his eyes closed and a little half smile on his face. He turned in a slow circle and waved his other hand as if he were greeting his adoring fans, which he was. One of the new waiters, a young kid, started to pull his phone out to take a picture or a video. Bryan reached over and pushed his hand back down. He shook his head. Seth's dance was just for them. It was not a thing to be shared."

Someone made a humming sound, like they were at church. Rachel couldn't tell who it was. The poet-woman? Don Blankman? Nancy's new boyfriend?

"Seth's dance was just for them, as some things are. No attempt to describe it would ever be enough. No video that went viral and spread around the world. Some things could not be translated and Seth's dance was one of these, plain and simple. 'Some things are just for us,' Bryan whispered to the new guy and he knew it was true."

The sound of laughter drifted in from the street. It was late and the Christmas lights that lined all the buildings downtown flickered on. During the pandemic, they'd decided to leave the lights up all year. Why not give themselves that pleasure?

"'I'm dancin' in the rain,' Seth said. He twirled the umbrella and did a slow-motion shuffle step. He tried to jump up and kick his heels together, but it didn't quite work. No one cared. That Wednesday, no one laughed. They watched Seth dance with absent smiles on their faces, smiles that were almost sad. They thought of watching old black-and-white movies with their kids during lockdown or of the time they'd got caught in the rain with the love of their life or of the satisfying space a good, dreary day provided to do nothing but catalog disappointments. They hoped Seth's dance would go on forever, but, of course, it could not. The door of the Saloon opened and customers came in, gazing around with puzzled looks, certain they had missed something important, which they had."

How long had she been reading? It felt like forever. Surely her time was already up, but the poet-woman still sat at her table, though she was no longer holding up her sign.

"But they also carried Seth's dancing with them through the rest of the shift. And maybe they carried it when they went home to someone waiting for them or to an empty room. The dance lived inside them. It wasn't much. But it was something."

Rachel stared down at that last sentence. God, it was horrible. She looked up and laughed. "That's it," she said.

The room erupted with applause. Rachel's little table of friends and family rose to their feet. Nancy whistled again. Even the poet-woman smiled. Rachel didn't deserve any of it, but she was grateful. "Thank you," she said. "Thanks."

Then it was over and everyone was filing outside into the dark.

"You were great," Charlie said.

"Is that about Joshua?" Sam asked.

"Sort of," Rachel said.

They gathered back at Rachel and Charlie's house, sitting in the backyard under the twinkle lights they'd strung during the pandemic. Charlie made all the drinks. "The talent doesn't mix cocktails," he declared as he filled glasses with ice.

Liz had brought a crown, which she placed on Rachel's head.

"That poet was such a taskmaster," Nancy said.

"She was okay," Rachel said.

She sat on her lounge chair, a gin martini in her hand. She was exhausted, but in a good way. She wasn't sure if she could ever do anything like that again. She listened to the conversations drifting around her.

"What did it all mean?" Loretta asked someone, but Rachel didn't hear the answer.

"Where's the kid?" Nancy asked her new boyfriend.

"Oh, he's got better things to do than to hang out with us," the boyfriend said.

"No, I think this is exactly how we're meant to live," Charlie was declaring from behind the makeshift bar they'd set up on the porch. "Small, dense settlements. Walkable. Surrounded by nature. The whole world should be built like Lanier."

"Did you hear some guy's opening a hot dog restaurant?" Sam was asking Liz. "Like, just, why?"

The moon shone, reflected in the window of the building next door. Their voices drifted up into the night sky, toward the church steeple and out over the river. The world had ended and they were still here. The world would end again. But for now, Rachel pulled the blanket up over her feet and took a sip of her martini, which was perfect.

She imagined walking through town in this sweet darkness, laying her hands on everything and everyone she loved. It was all within reach. It was all here. She could walk from one end of town to another in an hour's time, it was so small. But that wasn't right. It was so big. It was vast. A whole universe. Scarred. Wounded. Ugly. Full of beauty too big to fit inside any single human heart.

CAST OF CHARACTERS
(in alphabetical order)

Anna and Victoria and Jessie: Sam's roommates

Aunt Dora: Nancy's aunt

Aunt Gerdie: Loretta's aunt

Ava: Sam's girlfriend

Barry: the Parliament Funkadelic/James Brown/Harry Styles guy

Beth Clark: workshop leader and famous writer

Bethany: Don Blankmans' granddaughter

Blaine: boyfriend to Sam's mom/Charlie's ex-wife

Brady: Liz's son

Braxton: Sam's snooty ex-boyfriend

Bryan: Rachel's chill boss at the Main Street Saloon

Carol: boozehound and Joyce's friend

Celia: the hairdresser

Charlie: Rachel's husband and Sam's father

Christine Parker: wife of West Lanier's former pastor

Cindy Sawyer: Loretta's mother; liked cats

Craig: Tom's husband

Tom: Loretta's best friend and also friends with Charlie and Rachel

Daniel West Fortlow: hot dog guy; not balding; tall

Debra: Nancy's best friend

Don Blankman: savior of Lanier

Don Jr.: Don and Joyce's son

Dr. Barrett: Don's doctor in the Covid ward

Dr. Harvey: urologist and boyfriend to Nancy

Emily Butler: fellow painting student with Joyce

George Nordan: coffee shop regular and poet

Grandpa Joe: James's grandfather

Heather: Don and Joyce's daughter

Jackson: coffee shop regular and Don's Black friend

James: refugee from San Francisco

Jenny: realtor

Joshua: a waiter at the Main Street Saloon; cranky; dances

Joyce Blankman: Don's wife and aspiring artist

Julie Davis: Don's mistress and a nurse

The Kid where James mows lawns

Kyle: Nancy's grandson; Liz' son; dates Emily

Larry: Nancy's friend; husband to Max

Liz: daughter of Nancy; friend of Rachel; mother of Brady and Kyle

Loretta Sawyer: enemy of hot dog guys; friend to Tom and Rachel
    and Liz

Loretta's therapist

Lorn: newspaper delivery boy

Man with dog who walks like a cowboy

Max: Larry's husband

Mike Bowling: previous superintendent before Nancy

Nancy: Queen of the Black Sea; mother of Liz; friend to Debra;
    widow of Stan; also girlfriend of Dr. Harvey

Pam: odd talker and wife of Tony

Parrot Guy: also, sometimes kittens and ferrets

Pink Lady: no additional descriptions needed

Poet-woman: poetry night task-master

Rachel Barr: bartender; aspiring writer; wife to Charlie;
    stepmother to Sam; friend to Liz, Tom and Loretta
Rick: fellow painting student and husband to owner of a clothing
    store
Riverboat Nymphs: origins unknown
Ross: painting instructor
Sam: Rachel's stepdaughter; Charlie's daughter; girlfriend to Ava
Sandy: the high school guidance counselor
Shawnee: a waitress at the Main Street Saloon
Shay D: a drag performer
Stan: excellent dancer and late husband to Nancy
Susan: the Episcopal priest
Tom: Loretta's best friend from New York; husband to Craig; friend
    to Charlie and Rachel
Tony: Pam's husband
Workshop people: includes not-Emily and not-Pam

ACKNOWLEDGEMENTS

Thirty years ago, I was lucky enough to take a creative writing class taught by Clyde Edgerton, who wrote in his comments at the bottom of one of my stories, "If you keep writing, you will get published eventually." I was twenty-one, so the part of that sentence I paid attention to was the "you will get published." I skipped over the "if you keep writing" and the "eventually" bits. I didn't understand back then that those were the most important parts.

I did keep writing, with many interruptions along the way. I did *eventually* get published in a literary magazine, almost twenty years later. Anyway, thank you, Clyde, for those prophetic words, even if I didn't fully appreciate them at the time.

Thank you to everyone who expressed the least bit of faith in me and my writing over the years. It's a very long list. Writing, but especially publishing, is a cruel business. Every kind word is a lifeline. Thank you Greg Miller, for putting up with my precociousness as an undergrad. Thank you to all those literary magazines and journals that gave my work a chance over the years. Thank you to all the amazing writing workshops and conferences I learned from, including the Midwest Writers' Workshop and Writers in Paradise.

Thanks especially to the folks in the two workshops at Writers in Paradise who gave such helpful feedback on two of the stories from this collection. And to Elizabeth Strout and Stewart O'Nan, who led those amazing workshops, as well as Marina Pruna and all the other people who make that gorgeous week in St. Petersburg happen year after year. Thank you, also, Danielle Monroe for her careful reading and insight on these stories.

Thank you to my writing friend and pen pal Ellen Airgood. Thank you for the incredible generosity of agreeing to read a novel written by a complete and total stranger. Thank you for reading all the stories and novels and essays since then. Thank you for being my cheerleader and fellow traveler in this very weird and often bewildering world of writing and publishing.

I spent a lot of time alone with these stories, polishing them and adding to them. I knew that I was on the right track when I gave them to my forever-first-editor and he laughed the whole way through. Thanks, Jeff, for doing the dishes and cleaning the litter box and taking the trash out and making the cocktails and listening to me say the same thing about how messed up publishing is for the four millionth time without complaining and for all the other ways you make this writing life possible for me.

I have to admit that when I was writing the stories in this collection, I didn't much think they'd ever be published. They were too weird. Too small town. Too Midwestern. Too much inside the head of people that many of us would rather not spend time with. I thought they were the best writing I'd ever done and also that no one would probably ever read them. So a huge, enormous thank you to Henriette Lazaridis and Anjali Duva at Galiot Press for plucking this collection out of their slush pile and proving me wrong. Thank the universe for brave, creative women who are willing to take chances. For women who are willing to dream about how the world could be different and then make it happen. From the first conversation I had with Henriette and Anjali about what Galiot was trying to do, I was all in. Thank you Henriette, for your incredibly detailed and loving editing. And thanks to everyone else on the Galiot team for making this dream come true.

Thank you to Faceout Studios and the Galiot Press marketing team and to Euan Monaghan for the interior design.

In 2005, I bought an almost two hundred year old house in downtown Madison, Indiana. The town might have been the last place on the planet I would have ever picked to live (I mean, Indiana?) and yet it is simply the place I was always meant to be. It's the home I never knew I needed. When people in my life are unhappy, I cannot help but suggest they move to Madison, as if the town is a magical solution to all life's problems. It sort of was for me.

I can't thank everyone in Madison because the town may be small, but the list is long. Let me just say that writers may write alone, but there is always a community standing behind them. These stories are my love letter to Madison and all the people there. To the bartenders, the baristas, the waiters, the old guys sitting on the bench by the river, the women in the beauty salon, the goddesses. To the chocolate shop, the shoe store, the wine bar, the restaurant, the library, the bookstore. To the painters, the sculptors, the massage therapists, the artists, the musicians. And of course, my neighbors and my friends. Thank you for taking me in. Thank you for giving me a home. Thank you for gifting me with a lifetime of stories to tell.

ɟᴘ galiot press

Galiot's first three books were made possible in part
though the support of the following individuals:

Allison Cook & Jack Humphrey
Dena Enos
Marina Hatsopoulos
Bandita Joarder
Breanna Powers Kirk
Erin McKenna
Julia Sullivan
Justine Uhlenbrock

And 295 other contributors to
our crowdfunding campaign

For more about the author, additional content, and to look up or purchase additional Galiot books, visit **www.galiotpress.com**

Upcoming books:

SWALLOWTAIL by Emily Ross In Quincy, Massachusetts, a detective must unravel the mystery of her own abduction 20 years ago in order to find the killer of a local girl—before her own daughter is next. A literary mystery thriller steeped in imagery from Surrealist art and Greek mythology, SWALLOWTAIL is the moving story of a woman's journey to free herself from the trauma of her past, and a meditation on representations of women in the violence of myth and art. (Fall 2025)

BACKSTITCH by Marian Donahue Set in an art gallery in the Washington, DC, area, and structured as a journey through the gallery's rooms, BACKSTITCH is the story of two sisters who reunite at a retrospective of their troubled mother's art and must confront the consequences of her ambition and the difficult, private truths behind the family's public narrative. The novel is an exploration of family ties, the gift and cost of artistic talent, and the legacy that the artist's children must carry. (Spring 2026)